Neonatal Nurses

Sisters who save lives!

Sisters Penny and Alice love working together in
the Newborn Intensive Care Unit at Washington's
Wald Children's Hospital. Treating the hospital's
newest arrivals, Penny and Alice dedicate their
days and nights to their young patients. But is it
time that somebody dedicated their time to
Penny and Alice, too? Perhaps surgeon Benedict
and doctor Dougie might be just the men
to heal their neglected hearts!

Step into the world of these neonatal nurses with…

A Nurse to Claim His Heart by Juliette Hyland

Neonatal Doc on Her Doorstep by Scarlet Wilson

Available now!

Dear Reader,

It's always fun writing a duet with another medical romance author, and when I was asked to consider a sister story with fellow author Juliette Hyland, it was an instant yes!

There's fun in brainstorming the sisters, their characteristics and the men who will capture their hearts. I have the younger sister, Alice, and her slightly grumpy Scotsman, Dougie.

Both of my characters have secrets—parts of themselves they won't willingly reveal—and it takes a lot for them to finally get there. Here's hoping you enjoy the journey.

Love,

Scarlet Wilson

NEONATAL DOC
ON HER DOORSTEP

———

SCARLET WILSON

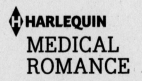

HARLEQUIN®
MEDICAL
ROMANCE™

Recycling programs
for this product may
not exist in your area.

ISBN-13: 978-1-335-40918-8

Neonatal Doc on Her Doorstep

Copyright © 2022 by Scarlet Wilson

Harlequin Enterprises ULC
22 Adelaide St. West, 41st Floor
Toronto, Ontario M5H 4E3, Canada
www.Harlequin.com

Printed in U.S.A.

Scarlet Wilson wrote her first story aged eight and has never stopped. She's worked in the health service for twenty years, having trained as a nurse and a health visitor. Scarlet now works in public health and lives on the West Coast of Scotland with her fiancé and their two sons. Writing medical romances and contemporary romances is a dream come true for her.

Books by Scarlet Wilson

Harlequin Medical Romance

The Christmas Project
A Festive Fling in Stockholm

Double Miracle at St. Nicolino's Hospital
Reawakened by the Italian Surgeon

Changing Shifts
Family for the Children's Doc

His Blind Date Bride
Marriage Miracle in Emergency

Visit the Author Profile page
at Harlequin.com for more titles.

To my partner in crime, Juliette Hyland.
Loved writing a duet with you, and thanks for the
expert knowledge of Washington and the use of
Foggy Bottom, which still makes me laugh!

CHAPTER ONE

ALICE GREENE LET out a sigh as her cat, Sooty, strode purposefully directly across her face for the third time. It was entirely deliberate. As soon as Sooty heard Alice's alarm, he wanted to ensure that Alice remembered to feed him before she left for work for the day.

'Once,' Alice muttered under the covers. 'Just once, I forgot. Do I get this treatment for the rest of my life?'

Sooty, pleased by the attention, let out a loud meow.

Alice sat up, throwing the covers off, and grabbed her clothes for work. She was in and out of the shower in five minutes—watched by Sooty in a lazy kind of way the whole time. 'This isn't a spectator sport,' she said under her breath as she pulled her clothes on and headed into the kitchen.

She pulled the cat food from the cupboard and put a small cup's worth in Sooty's food bowl, refreshing his water too, then giving Sooty an affectionate rub at the back of his neck as he immediately started to eat.

Her little rescue black cat with a smudge of white on his coat was her only company these days. Not that she minded. Her sister, Penny, had found her happy ever after with one of the doctors they worked with at Wald Children's Hospital and Alice was happy for her. She was. Benedict Denbar had made Penny's eyes sparkle in a way that Alice had never seen before. They'd got engaged and Penny had moved in with him, leaving Alice alone in the townhouse they'd shared in Washington.

It was fine. She just needed someone else to cover half the rent, and one of her colleagues from the NICU where she worked, Mariela Martínez, was due to move in.

It would be odd sharing a home with someone other than her sister. They'd shared a room for most of their childhood, moving every three to five years since their parents were in the Army. Alice had always considered Penny her best friend, and had even followed her into nursing.

She smiled as she picked up her backpack and headed to the Metro. Penny was working today. They'd maybe even be able to have breakfast together and catch up.

Her phone buzzed as she took the short walk to the station. Alice read the message via her dating app and shook her head. Nope. Two dates with the guy she'd nicknamed the 'handsome spook' were enough. That was the thing about Washington. There were plenty of men. But the majority of them fell into two categories—members of the intelligence community, or ties with politics. It was all getting boring. The guys who worked for the intelligence agencies seemed to have a permanent level of mistrust about them, and the ones with the political ties all appeared to like talking—mainly about themselves.

Alice wanted someone fun. Someone different. Someone who didn't treat her as if she might look good on their arm. Someone who might look at her the way Benedict looked at her sister.

It was odd. For years she'd been the dating queen. Never too serious about anyone— always getting out before feelings could be hurt. Or at least she'd tried to.

But around two years ago—right at the time Penny had found out her ex-fiancé actually had a wife and family—Alice had found herself in a sticky situation with a guy she'd dated for around six weeks. After weeks of late-night calls and strange stuff around the townhouse, she'd finally spoken to a friend of hers who was a DC cop. He'd called it stalking, and had a serious conversation with the guy, who'd sworn that Alice had encouraged him and given him a whole host of signals that she wanted the relationship to continue, and to be serious.

She hadn't. But it had made her re-evaluate almost every word she said on a date, and every single text that she sent. She never wanted to be accused of mixed signals again. She hadn't even told Penny about it at the time. She'd been staying in Ohio with her then fiancé and had enough problems of her own without Alice adding to them. And by the time Penny had dumped her ex, and moved back to Washington, everything had been over, so there didn't seem any point in bringing it up. Penny would just have worried anyhow. And at twenty-nine Alice was big enough to look after herself.

It had unsettled her. Her colleagues at work made fun of her dating apps without realising it allowed her to tell others she was looking for love, while keeping all men at a distance.

She sighed as she reached Foggy Bottom station and descended on the escalator to wait for the train. She'd spent the last few days at the NICU looking after twins. Born at twenty-four weeks, and both struggling. Years ago, babies this small wouldn't have stood a chance. But technology and medicine had long since adapted to the special needs of premature babies. Nowadays, chances for babies like these could be good—even if they needed a prolonged stay in NICU until they were ready for discharge. NICU nurses like Alice spent just as much time caring for the parents of her small babies as she did caring for the babies. Most of the parents were un-prepared for their early deliveries—or had barely had a few days' notice. Ruby and Ry-an's mom was certainly in the unprepared category. Alice was worried about her. She still seemed shell-shocked. It wasn't unusual. But it had been nearly a week now, and Angie still seemed distant. She'd mentioned a type of candy that was her favourite. Maybe Alice could try and pick it up for her at the station near the hospital—maybe even a coffee too. Anything to try and engage with Angie a lit-tle more and try to connect with her.

The ringtone of 'The Power of Love' by Huey Lewis sounded and she pulled her phone from her pocket, smiling. Today's tune was from the *Back to the Future* movie.

She'd keep it until a workmate could work out what movie it was from, and then change to another. It was like a mini competition and Alice had a world of tunes from eighties movies lined up on her phone. She wrinkled her brow as she saw her workmate Mariela's name light up on her screen. Mariela wasn't working today, and Alice knew her well enough to know she wasn't normally an early riser.

She didn't waste time. 'What's up? Everything okay?'

Mariela's heavily accented voice seemed to rush out a thousand words at once and, coupled with the background noise of the Metro, Alice only caught fragmented parts. 'Mamá…accident…return to Spain…sorry.'

Alice struggled to hear, concentrating as best she could. Her mind was racing. 'Do you need me to do anything to help you?'

Mariela was clearly understandably upset and Alice hated to hear her friend and workmate like this. Her brain started to claw at another tiny idea, but she pushed it aside to concentrate on what her friend was telling her.

'I think it will be months, not weeks. So I'm sorry to let you down, Alice, but I just don't know if or when I'll get back to

Washington—' Her voice broke and Alice broke in.

'Mariela. Don't worry about that. Don't give it a second thought. Save all your energy for getting home and seeing your mamá. That's what matters now. I wish I could come and give you a big hug. I love you, honey. And I'm sending up prayers for you and your family.'

Mariela gave another sob. 'Thank you— and tell my babies that I'm sorry—and all our parents.'

By the time she finished the call, Alice felt wrung out. She stopped on automatic pilot and picked up a coffee for herself, her sister and for Angie, along with a multitude of candy bars for them all. Chocolate was needed at times like this.

Her head was swimming. By the time she reached NICU and stowed her bag and jacket in her locker, she could tell her workmates already knew about Mariela's mother's accident.

Hushed voices were whispering. 'It doesn't sound too good. I hope Mariela is going to be okay.'

'Can we put our heads together and cover all her shifts on a temporary basis? Does anyone mind?'

There were lots of shaking heads.

Alice took a few moments to wash her hands and then go over to Angie, who was sitting in a comfortable chair between the two NICU cribs for her babies. She looked a little stunned when Alice handed her the coffee and a selection of candy. 'I remembered you said the other day that you liked these.'

Angie's eyes were wide and she nodded at the whispering staff. 'What's wrong? Has something happened to one of the babies?'

Alice quickly put her hand on Angie's. 'No, not at all.' She shouldn't be surprised. The parents who spent a long time in the NICU often picked up on things—and it was only natural for Angie to think the concerns were around a fellow patient.

All staff business was usually kept out of NICU, but the truth was they were all like family in here. Keeping secrets might add to Angie's worry that they were keeping something from her.

Alice shook her head. 'Mariela—the nurse who has worked with Ruby and Ryan?'

Angie nodded.

'She's heading back to Spain. Her mom has been in a road traffic accident and is in hospital. She just phoned to let us all know. The staff are just trying to cover her shifts—and they're worried for her. That's all.'

The sigh of relief was audible to them both, but Angie was instantly embarrassed and started talking quickly. 'She's such a nice girl. Is it serious? It must be if they've called her back to Spain.'

Alice bit her lip. 'We don't know all the details. So, in the meantime, we'll just all cross our fingers.'

It wasn't entirely true. Mariela's mother had sustained a serious head injury and several broken bones. But Alice didn't need to share that.

'She wanted me to tell you that she was sorry she had to leave you, Ruby and Ryan.'

'She did?'

Alice nodded. She could finally start to see some little connections being made with Angie. A quick glance at both babies' charts told her their condition was both steady. Babies in NICU could deteriorate at a moment's notice, so she never took anything for granted.

'Drink your coffee and I'll be back to help you take care of Ruby and Ryan once I've had the handover report.'

Angie gave a nod and settled back in her chair. Her skin was pale and she was clearly tired. Sleeping in a NICU was virtually impossible. It didn't matter that the myriad of beeping monitors were kept at a low level to protect the tiny babies. Parents in here were tuned into the smallest noise, their senses already on overload at being introduced to the scary, unfamiliar environment. It didn't matter that there were plenty of side rooms with proper beds for the parents to sleep in if they chose. Most didn't. And most looked similar to Angie.

Alice made her way over to the nurses' station. Tara, the charge nurse, was talking in a low voice, first running through every patient, stats, test results awaited, then giving any concerns—both about baby and about parents. When she'd finished she nodded at the rota showing on the nearby monitor. 'I've spoken to HR. Mariela will be having two weeks' leave, then will likely go onto unpaid leave for a few months. I'll see if we can get some cover. But you know how hard that is around here.'

They all nodded. Although the unit was generally kept in a quiet and smooth-functioning manner, no one could hide the emotional impact working in a place like this had on staff. Lots of staff only lasted a few years in a place like this. Losing tiny babies was devastating to the staff as well as the parents.

'Just let us know when you need cover.' Penny was at Alice's elbow. 'We can all pitch in,' she said sincerely.

Alice grinned at her. 'Your new fiancé might not like you volunteering to spend extra hours in the NICU.'

Penny shook her head. 'My new fiancé will likely be here himself, so it's fine.'

Benedict was one of the doctors in the NICU and had a strong work ethic, so Alice didn't doubt her sister's words for a second.

He appeared as if by magic behind them. 'Talking about me again?' He smiled. He nudged Alice. 'Watch out, I'll start to think my future sister-in-law might actually like me.'

Alice rolled her eyes, ignoring the buzz from her scrubs. It was likely another notification from the dating app.

'You gonna get that?' Benedict asked.

Alice shook her head. 'I'm on duty. No time for phones. Anyhow, I need to spend the next few hours finding myself a new housemate. Know anyone looking for a place?'

Benedict frowned for a second, then it was almost as if she could see the dots connecting. 'Oh, of course, I hadn't even thought of that.'

Penny reached over and put her hand on her sister's elbow. 'You know I'll help out. I don't want to see you stuck for rent.'

Alice waved her hand. Penny had only just moved in with Benedict—the last thing she wanted to do was spoil her sister's deserved happiness.

She held out her hands. 'This is a giant hospital. There must be someone around here who is looking for a perfectly hospitable, completely house-trained and well-behaved housemate.'

Benedict folded his arms, a look of amusement written all over his face as he exchanged glances with Penny. 'Wow, don't know who they might be, but I'd like to meet them.'

'I'll crack the jokes,' said Alice as she moved off, heading back to Angie and the twins. Her mind was churning. She wasn't exactly penniless. She did have an emergency stash, but she'd rather not dip into it. She'd rather find a housemate. But she wasn't desperate either. Mariela was a friend who she knew well. Agreeing to share with her had been an easy option. She'd heard too many horror tales of unknown housemates with a whole host of weird habits moving into shared properties.

The house that she'd shared with her sister was actually somewhere she loved. When she'd found the townhouse to rent in the Foggy Bottom neighbourhood of Washington she couldn't have been more delighted. The area got its name from the morning mist that rose off its southern boundary at the Potomac River. But the neighbourhood stretched right up to the West End and included the Kennedy Center for Performing Arts, a boat centre, the George Washington University Museum, the gorgeous green space of Rock Creek Park and, of course, the White House. There were a huge array of restaurants, hotels and bars. And, with the university so close, it meant the international students from across the globe lived in the accommodation nearby, giving a real community feel to the neighbourhood. The fact it was in easy walking distance of the Metro made it even better for early-morning starts or late-night finishes.

Her townhouse was bright and airy, with white walls, wooden floors throughout and an open-plan kitchen/living area on one floor. Two bedrooms and two bathrooms upstairs gave her plenty of living space, but she still was uneasy about sharing her space with someone she didn't know.

As she made her way back to Angie she noticed that the young mum was looking a little brighter. Maybe the candy and coffee pick-me-up had been a good idea. Alice would do anything she could to support her patient, hoping that, in turn, it would help Angie relax a little in the unit, and maybe become more attached to her babies.

Alice pushed all thoughts about the townhouse out of her head. Angie, Ruby and Ryan were her priority for the next few hours and they would be getting her complete and undivided attention.

Dougie MacLachlan groaned as he stared at the black door in front of him. 'Could this day get any worse?' He said the words out loud, even though no one else was listening.

He hadn't slept in two days. His first flight from Glasgow to London had been delayed, meaning he'd missed his flight to Washington and had to be rerouted. Then one of the rerouted flights had engine trouble and he'd ended up at a US airport he'd never even heard of, with even more difficulties getting to Washington. Now, it seemed the place he'd rented online had double-booked him and another couple for the same apartment. And they'd arrived first, leaving Dougie with no place to stay in a city that was completely unfamiliar to him.

He'd called the rental agency three times. A 'technical error' had been the first explanation. But when it turned out they couldn't find him another place today he'd used some pretty colourful Scottish language.

He'd dragged two huge suitcases up three flights of stairs, and now he'd have to drag them back down. The couple who'd reached the apartment before him had been quietly smug. It hadn't helped.

He glanced at his watch. Having lost more than twenty-four hours along this journey, he was due to start work in the next hour.

He ignored his aching shoulders and his rumbling stomach and headed back to the Metro. The job at Wald Children's had come up at just the right time. It was a teaching hospital—just like the one he'd come from in London, and previously in Glasgow, and was considered to be one of the top NICUs in the country.

After a difficult year, he'd jumped at the chance of a change of scenery and a change of faces. But the one thing he wouldn't compromise on was his specialty. Dougie had fallen in love with the idea of working in a NICU before he'd even started as a medical student. Lots of people shied away from delivering specialist care to these tiny patients. But from the first moment he'd stepped inside a NICU he'd known this was where he wanted to work. Everything else had just been a path to his specialty.

He'd grown up in one of the rougher parts of Glasgow. Whilst other people might paint a dark picture of the area, Dougie had been raised in a community where people looked out for each other and walked freely in and out of each other's houses. He'd been bright, and his friends and family had all encouraged him to study. University tuition fees were covered for Scottish students, and medicine had been within his reach.

It had been quite a shock when, the day after he'd celebrated his exam results and acceptance into medical school, his childhood friend Lisa had gone into labour. Her hidden pregnancy and subsequent lack of antenatal care had haunted him ever since, and when she'd delivered her daughter at twenty-eight weeks Dougie had been one of the people who'd sat with her through the last few weeks of the summer in the sweltering NICU.

He'd been fascinated—trying to drink in

as much knowledge as possible, while understanding the confusion, guilt and fatigue of his childhood friend. His goddaughter Trixie was now a healthy fourteen-year-old who could literally talk for Scotland and she made every day brighter. She'd made him follow her on all the latest social media channels and regularly filmed clips of herself and her friends dancing in various parts of the city to the latest tunes—usually in some kind of costume. So far they had been clowns, zombies, nuns and priests, rival football teams and finally gangsters. Dougie couldn't keep up. Truth was he was scared to. If he stayed still long enough she might try and drag him into one of those fifteen-second dance clips, and Dougie had as much natural rhythm as a kitten in clogs.

He sighed and started dragging his suitcases down the stairs and back to the Metro, which was more crowded than before. Peak travel time. Great. Just what he needed.

By the time he reached Wald's all he wanted to do was dump his bags and find a corner to crawl into—preferably a corner with food.

But this was his first day in a new job, and Dougie was old enough to know that first impressions counted. He dragged his cases to Admin, then HR, signing everything required and getting a formal ID. If the staff were surprised at his rumpled jeans and T-shirt that he'd travelled in, they were polite enough not to mention it.

Four wrong turns later, he still hadn't found the staff changing room. Worse than that, the smell of cooked food was drifting tantalisingly along a corridor somewhere. Normal people were clearly eating breakfast.

After dragging his cases past the large sign to the NICU for the fifth time, he gave up and used his new ID to scan entry.

Heads looked up as he dragged his cases in behind him and dumped them to the side. Coffee. He could smell coffee somewhere.

A slim nurse with dark hair in a high ponytail and bright pink scrubs moved away from a NICU crib, her head slightly tilted.

'Can I help you?' She was noticeably scanning his body. In his brain-addled confusion he wondered if she was about to say something about his rumpled state or if she was checking him out, before he realised exactly what she was looking for—an ID badge.

He pulled it from the pocket of his jeans. 'Douglas MacLachlan. I'm your new doctor. I was trying to get changed and then report to Benedict Denbar. But someone decided to hide the changing rooms from me.'

There was the hint of a smirk. She gave a nod. 'Alice Greene. NICU nurse.' She raised her eyebrows just a touch. 'Having a bad day?'

He resisted the temptation to snap. He was tired. He was grouchy. He just wanted to get this day started so he could hopefully reach the other end without slumping in a corner. If he ever found the changing rooms in this place, at this rate it was likely to be where he would spend the night.

An older blonde woman appeared with her brow furrowed. 'Alice, it's time for your break. Why don't you try and sort out our new doc?'

Dougie straightened up. 'I've still to report to Benedict Denbar.'

The woman waved her hand. 'Don't worry about that. I'll tell Benedict you're around.' She glanced at the cases. 'And we try not to encourage our staff to move right in.'

As if his humiliation wasn't complete, his stomach gave a loud grumble. He opened his mouth to reply, but Alice had moved next to him and gave him an unexpected nudge. 'Tara's our charge nurse. Her word is law. Let's go.'

As he made a grab for his cases again, Alice held open the door for him. She couldn't hide the amusement on her face as she led him down a corridor that seemed familiar. 'Here—' she pointed '—locker rooms. But I can tell you right now. There's no locker big enough for those cases.'

He sighed, not even wanting to start to explain. 'Thanks. Are there showers in there?'

She nodded. 'Want me to grab you something from the canteen while you shower?'

He hesitated. It was a nice offer. But he'd only just met this nurse. He shook his head. 'Thanks, but no. I'll get showered and changed and head back to the NICU.'

'Do you have your own scrubs?'

It was a completely normal question. A lot of staff who'd worked in NICUs for years wore their own distinctive scrubs. But for some reason it threw him. His mind couldn't quite find the answer.

She gave a little shake of her head. 'No matter, but if you don't, the laundry trolley with towels and fresh scrubs is on the left-hand side of the room.'

Before he had a chance to form words, she strolled down the corridor in the direction of the food he was craving but had been too proud to ask for.

Darn it. Dougie flung the door to the locker room open, instantly flinching when it banged off the wall behind. He glanced around quickly, relieved to find the room was currently empty. He did have scrubs in one of his cases, but he had no idea which one and he didn't feel inclined to open them and start rifling through them right now.

There was a stack of blue scrubs on the linen trolley that Alice had directed him to, so he grabbed a set, along with a towel, and headed to the showers.

His skin was instantly relieved by the rush of hot water on his skin, and he scrubbed himself briskly with the shower gel on the wall, washing away any aromas or sweat he'd picked up on his long travels. As he washed his face he realised he hadn't had the chance to shave. By the time he'd found his shaving gear and started it would all take far too long. So Dougie just closed off the shower, dried off and pulled on the scrubs. At least he felt a bit more awake and his brain less foggy. He'd needed that.

He put his wallet, passport and other valuables in one of the lockers and walked back out of the room into the bright corridor. It was currently quiet, so for one minute he closed his eyes, put his hands on his hips and arched his back, stretching it out to try and work out all the knots that had formed from sitting in uncomfortable airport seats and cramped plane rows.

'This some kind of pre-match warm-up?' came the amused American voice.

Alice had reappeared and was carrying a brown paper bag and a takeaway cup.

'What?' Not the politest reply, but he was getting tired of being this staff member's entertainment. He hadn't paid much attention earlier, but now they were out of the unit in the bright fresh lights in the corridor Alice Greene was more than a little eye-catching.

Her dark hair swung in a ponytail, held in place by some bright, crinkly thing that would look more appropriate in a disco. She had clear skin, full lips and brown eyes that seemed to have very long eyelashes.

She laughed as she looked at him and pushed the cup and bag towards him. 'Don't you have wrestling in Scotland? You looked like you were doing a pre-match warm-up. Anyhow, I know you said you didn't want anything, but you seemed kinda cranky, so I got you some food.'

As he took the offered items she didn't wait to see what he would say, just kept walking back towards the unit.

'Thank you,' he called after her, a bit later than he should have.

She glanced over her shoulder. 'Try and crack a smile,' she said. 'That cool Scottish accent will only work for so long.'

He breathed, inhaling the coffee and taking a sip. The bag was a different story. He looked cautiously inside. A bagel and cream cheese. Not his first choice. But beggars couldn't be choosers.

What did she mean—'crack a smile'? Was he coming over as grumpy? He wasn't trying to, but the last twenty-four hours had just been one disaster after another. As for the accent comment, he'd have to think about that one later. He watched her swaying hips for a moment before realising what he was doing and gave himself a shake. His stomach gave another growl and he knew it was time to concentrate on the food. He'd taken two bites before he was even near the NICU again and was finished long before he walked through the door.

A tall man with dark skin looked up and gave a beaming smile. 'Dr MacLachlan, come on over.'

It was the first spark of joy that he'd felt since getting here. By this point, Dougie was clearly a bit late—but this guy seemed totally chilled about it. Maybe he'd heard the suitcase story.

They shook hands warmly as Benedict introduced himself. He was clearly as passionate about his role as Dougie was. He showed him around the unit, logged him into the electronic systems and gave him a crash course in ordering tests and reviewing results. He gave him his pager, showed him the on-call rota and introduced him to as many people as possible. Dougie was feeling a bit more awake, and did his best to remember everything he was being told. He'd really have liked to scribble a few notes, but didn't want to seem as if he couldn't remember simple facts.

The NICU layout was familiar, as were most of the protocols and procedures. Once he was finally left to his own devices, Dougie took a bit of time to go through the current patients' records. A few babies in here had reached their hundred-day milestone. Whilst in some ways it was a cause for celebration, it was also a clear indication of how sick some of these babies had been.

Dougie blinked as a woman in patterned scrubs appeared in front of him. 'Pleased to meet you, Dr MacLachlan, I'm Penny Greene.'

The expression on his face must have said

it all. At first, he'd thought Alice was joking with him and had just changed scrubs. But after a few seconds he realised this was an entirely different person. The nurse laughed and waved a hand. 'Yes, she's my sister. And yes, some people think we look like twins, but I promise you we are very different.' She leaned over and whispered, 'I'll give you a hint; we have different coloured eyes.'

Dougie reached over and shook her hand, taking in her blue eyes, just as Benedict moved back over and gave her a nudge with his hip. 'Dr MacLachlan's got more pressing worries than telling the two of you apart. I hear he's got house troubles.'

There was something in the way they stood close and looked at each other that told him these two were very familiar with each other.

Penny's eyes widened. 'What do you mean, you've got house trouble?'

Dougie sighed. 'The place I was supposed to be renting was double-booked. My flights were delayed and rerouted, which meant that by the time I arrived the other people had already arrived and had moved in. It seems that finders are keepers.'

Penny shook her head. 'That's ridiculous. Did you contact the rental company?'

He nodded. 'Seems like I've moved to

Washington in prime season. They couldn't guarantee they could find me another place.'

'So what are you going to do?' Penny gave a strange glance at Benedict.

'I guess I'll need to find a hotel for the night and try and sort it out in the next few days.' The mere thought of it made him tired. 'Know any hotels close by?'

Alice came over and handed a chart to Benedict, which he glanced at and signed electronically. He could hear the sound of a phone vibrating in her pocket but she ignored it. Dougie shifted uncomfortably, watching as Alice moved to the drug trolley and started drawing up medicine. Things seemed very casual around here.

Penny pressed her lips together. 'I might know somewhere that you could rent at short notice.' She hesitated for a split second. 'As long as you don't mind sharing.'

'My only criteria right now is somewhere that has a bed.'

Penny gave Benedict that look again, then they both turned their heads to Alice, who was locking the drug cupboard with her medicines stored in a disposable tray.

As if she sensed their gazes, she looked up. 'What?'

'Dr MacLachlan is stranded,' said Penny. 'He has nowhere to stay.'

Something flickered behind Alice's eyes. She looked over at Dougie and shook her head. 'No,' she said without thinking. She even took a step back.

Benedict moved over and beamed at her. 'Come on, Alice. It's perfect timing. You need someone to rent a room at your town-house, and Dr MacLachlan is looking for somewhere to stay.'

'Dougie,' he said automatically. He didn't want everyone to spend all their time calling him Dr MacLachlan. He shifted his shoulders uncomfortably. This was all getting incredibly awkward incredibly quickly.

'He's grumpy,' she went on.

'I'm not grumpy,' he retorted.

Alice waved her hand. 'Well, you were definitely hangry then.'

'I'm not any more, though, thanks to you.'

She stared at him. He stared back.

He wanted to laugh out loud. How on earth had he got himself in this position? He didn't want to share a place with someone from his brand-new NICU.

'I don't even know him. He might have bad habits.'

This was like a playground fight.

'It's fine. I'll find a place to stay. I'm sure it won't take long. The rental agency might come through for me.' He pulled his phone from his pocket, silently praying that he'd missed a call, a text or an email. His phone screen was annoyingly blank.

'Don't give it a thought,' he continued. 'Last place I want to go is someplace that I'm not welcome.'

Alice flinched as if she'd been stung. 'Brutal,' she said quickly.

He had a horrible feeling that as workmates they weren't going to get along at all.

Then she let out a sigh and folded her arms. 'Do you smoke?'

'No.'

'Do you have weird music taste?'

He almost laughed at the bizarre question. 'No.'

'Do you leave everything at your backside?'

This time he did burst out laughing. 'I haven't heard that expression in years! And no, my mother trained me well. I do know how to pick up after myself.'

Alice shrugged and pointed at her chest. 'Army brat. Not many places we haven't lived. I've picked up lots of expressions.'

Her sister moved over next to her. 'Go on, Alice. It will help you out of a bind.'

A look of annoyance flickered over Alice's face.

'I can bake. Red velvet muffins are my speciality,' said Dougie. He was actually enjoying the toing and froing. He got the impression that, although she'd been caught unawares, she wasn't entirely as inhospitable as she was acting. The last thing he'd ever want to do was be an unwelcome guest in someone's home.

Her eyebrows lifted. 'How about banana loaf?'

He nodded. Not entirely sure he could. But anyone could search a recipe.

'Do you like cats?'

This could be a trick question. He wouldn't put it past her. But he pasted a smile on his face because this answer was going to be true. 'I like cats, but cats *adore* me.'

She looked at him suspiciously. 'I'll give you a week's trial.'

A week. That would give him enough time to read the riot act to the rental agency and give them a chance to make up for their mistake. He tried to ignore the fact that they hadn't seemed too bothered at all this morning about their error.

'A week's trial is generous,' he said, not even trying to pretend that every muscle in his body wasn't relaxing at the thought of having somewhere to put his head down tonight. 'Thank you.'

She picked up the drug tray and wagged her finger at him. 'Don't make me regret it.' She moved across the unit and back to the babies in her care.

'Perfect,' Penny said, smiling. She seemed relieved. And Dougie wondered if he should ask why.

Benedict handed him some notes. 'I'd like you to review these patients so we can have a chat about them later at our NICU hub meeting.'

Dougie nodded and took the names of the babies offered. He was used to working this way. It wasn't unusual for staff to gather and review patients together. Often opinions from all staff helped—other NICU specialists, nurses and doctors could give insights and encourage a whole team approach. As Dougie scanned the notes and records the hairs on the back of his neck started to prickle.

No, he told himself. *Stop it*. There was no reason to start with thoughts like that. This was Washington, not London. An entirely new city, and an entirely fresh start.

And he tried to keep that firmly in his head for the rest of the day. He couldn't let the demons of the past destroy his future.

CHAPTER TWO

IT WASN'T UNTIL a few hours later that Dougie finally realised he had no idea what kind of place Alice lived in, how far away it was, how much the rent was, or any of the important things he likely should have asked.

When his shift finished he handed over to the on-call doctor. He felt a little more comfortable now. In the last few hours he'd tried to familiarise himself with as many of the systems and procedures as possible. All while secretly auditing them in his head for any possible flaws. But systems seemed good here. Guidelines and safety signs were visible all around the NICU. The emergency trolley was clearly labelled. All equipment stowed safely, and drug keys kept by the nurse in charge of the unit. He hadn't spotted anything that gave him cause for concern.

When he finally let go of his thoughts, he saw Alice pacing near the door and realised she must be waiting for him. He strode quickly across the unit.

'Sorry, let me just grab my things.'

He felt like a teenager who'd missed their curfew by the look she gave him and hurried to the changing rooms to throw on his clothes and grab his suitcases. The coffee and food throughout the day, as well as the introduction to a new unit, had wakened up his sleep-deprived brain, but as soon as they stepped out into the warm evening air it was like being hit by a tidal wave of jetlag.

Alice gave him a sideways glance. 'Give me one of those cases.'

He shook his head. 'It's fine.'

'It's not fine, Douglas. You look like death warmed over.' Her warm hand reached over, brushing against his, and took it firmly from his hands.

He took a few missteps then shook his head, a tired smile on his face. 'It's not Douglas. It's Dougie.'

Her eyebrows arched. She let out a half-laugh.

'What?'

'It's just the way you say it. It sounds so… Scottish. Doog-hee.' She drew out the sounds.

Dougie shot her an unimpressed glance. 'Maybe it sounds Scottish because it is, and

so am I. And it's not Doog-hee. It's Dougie,'
he said, knowing it sounded identical to the
way she'd just drawled out his name, but entirely ignoring that fact.

'Right.' Alice's one-word answer told him
to give up now.

They reached the Metro and he glanced at
the stairs. 'It's only a few stops,' Alice said
over her shoulder.

He felt around his pockets, praying he
could find some change. He'd changed money
but had made the mistake of not asking for a
mix of notes, meaning most of his cash was
in hundred dollar bills.

'I'll get it,' she said. She was beginning to
look a little exasperated with him. And he got
it. He did. He'd been pushed on her by her sister for reasons unknown to him. But he was
too tired and didn't feel as if he should spend
the whole time apologising to her.

'Thanks,' he murmured as they headed to
a platform, where the train came along a few
moments later. She was true to her word and
a few stops later they came out at another
station.

Dougie blinked as he looked at the sign. It
was as if he'd stepped out into some surreal
dream. Maybe he'd fallen asleep on the train?
'You've got be joking?'

'What?' asked Alice as she dragged his suitcase along the platform, the wheels making an unhealthy noise.

'Foggy Bottom?' He couldn't believe he was saying the words. 'This place is called Foggy Bottom?' He started laughing, a belly laugh that bubbled up from deep inside him.

Alice gave a wave of her hand as if she'd heard all this a million times before. 'Yeah, so what? It's famous. Haven't you heard of it?'

But he was still laughing, imagining his childhood friends back in Scotland if they'd known that such a place existed. It didn't matter how juvenile it was. He was always going to find this funny.

He kept staring at the sign as he pulled his other case along, almost running straight into the back of Alice.

'Are you done now?' she asked angrily.

'Probably not,' he admitted. 'This would be hours of fun back in Scotland.'

'I wouldn't come to Scotland and make fun of the places that you live in.'

'Didn't you just make fun of how I say my name?'

There was a few seconds' silence. She blew a piece of hair from her face, looking annoyed. 'Touché,' she finally said, before turning and heading for the exit.

He dragged his case along silently, secretly wanting to ask how far it was to her place, but not wanting to give her the satisfaction.

When she finally stopped at the entrance of a smart townhouse he was pleasantly surprised. Inside, the white walls, wooden floors and open-plan style gave a real sense of space. The kitchen and living areas blended into one, with plenty of windows to let in light. The whole home was clean and comfortable and he sent a silent prayer upwards after his earlier experiences.

'Bedrooms are upstairs,' she said. 'Yours will be the one on the right. It's got its own bathroom, but we need to share the space down here. Do you want something to eat?'

He looked over at her in surprise that she was being hospitable. There had been an uncomfortable edge to Alice ever since she'd agreed to let him stay. Truth was, he still planned on looking for somewhere else.

'You don't need to feed me,' he said, truly not wishing to be any more trouble.

She opened her cupboards and the first thing that struck was how bare they were. 'I'm not really the plan ahead type,' she said. 'I have—' she held up one hand '—noodles or popcorn.' She put down the packets and opened the fridge. 'Or eggs, some salad and strawberries.'

'Eggs and strawberries,' he repeated. 'Interesting combination.'

She gave a shrug. 'It's not like I knew I was about to have a new guest.'

'Someone else from NICU was supposed to be moving in with you?'

'Yeah.' Alice gave a sigh. 'But Mariela is a foodie. She would have moved in with a load of groceries to make great Italian foods. To be honest, I was kinda counting on it.'

He nodded understandingly. 'To be honest too, Alice, I'm knackered. But I'd like to eat something before I go to bed. How about we pick up some takeaway? I saw a pizza place just down the street.' He looked down at his clothes. 'How about we get changed and head out?'

Alice actually looked relieved. 'Sure, give me five minutes.'

Dougie lifted both cases and carried them up the stairs. The bedroom was bigger than he'd expected. It had the same pale wood floor and a large bed with white bedding that looked good enough just to flop on. There was plenty of cupboard and drawer space and he opened his first suitcase and grabbed out some jeans and a T-shirt. His wash bag was near the top so he carried his things into the en suite bathroom and washed his face and hands, brushing his teeth and changing his clothes. It was odd what a relief it was to put his things somewhere—even if it was temporary.

As he turned around he realised there was a bunch of bright pink flowers in a short white vase on the window ledge. Alice must have bought them for her colleague who should have moved in. It was a nice touch and even though he sensed she didn't appreciate the situation he hoped he'd be able to make sure they could be comfortable around each other.

As he looked about the room the door opened slightly and a black cat with a white smudge wandered in, eyeing him suspiciously. He bent down and gave the cat a scratch. It kept staring at him with wary eyes but didn't move away. 'Hi there,' he said softly.

He splashed some water through his hair, dampening down the slight curl. He'd need to find a barber in the city at some point.

The cat had now jumped on his bed with an air of superiority and curled up where his pillow was. Dougie shook his head and smiled. With one final glance at the bed, he made his way back downstairs.

* * *

Alice was still questioning all this. She was sure this new Scottish doctor was fine. But she'd wanted to share her place with someone that she knew and trusted. Someone who wouldn't care if they caught her in her underwear or nightclothes walking through the house en route to raid the kitchen. It didn't help that she found the accent sexy, or that she'd noticed just how attractive Douglas— no, Dougie—actually was.

Did he have a girlfriend, a fiancée, a wife? She hadn't noticed a ring but presumed if he were married he might have brought his wife with him.

'Hey.' His footsteps sounded on the stairs and she tried not to notice he'd changed into black jeans and a black T-shirt that showed off his build and made him look like some kind of movie star. Great. 'I met your cat.'

'Sooty. Wondered where he'd gone. Did he scratch you?'

He shook his head. 'Not at all. He's curled up on the bed as if he owns the place.'

'He does…kinda. If he doesn't like you— we'll know soon.'

Dougie gave a maddeningly easy smile. 'I told you. Cats love me.'

She wasn't entirely sure if he was being serious or not. But at the end of the day Sooty would let him know who was boss.

'Let me pick the pizza place,' she said quickly.

'Of course,' he said. 'You know everywhere. And I'll try and pick up some groceries tomorrow.'

She should have planned better. If Mariela had been moving in, they would likely have gone grocery shopping together once Alice had got home from work. But it hardly seemed like the thing to suggest to a guy who was clearly tired and had two large cases to battle through the Washington Metro.

As they walked along the street it was clear Dougie was taking in all his surroundings. 'Which way to the White House? Where's the George Washington Museum?' The stream of questions was endless. She pointed out a few other places. 'The area down there is mainly full of tourists, the food places overpriced. If you go down that way, there's a wholefoods place and a few market stores, and another block down there's a great place for bread and desserts.

'If you want clothes stores, you'll have to go into the city centre. There's an open-air plaza there with a lot of high-end stores.'

Dougie just gave a nod as he kept looking about. 'Just trying to get my bearings,' he said.

She gave him a sideways glance. 'You said something earlier...knockered?'

He laughed. 'Knackered. Good Scots word. Tired—actually, it really means more than tired. It basically means you could sleep on the edge of a cliff.'

'How come you're so tired?'

He sighed. 'My plane from Scotland was delayed, meaning I missed my flight from London. Then they rerouted me, but that flight had engine trouble and we had to reroute again. I was travelling for more than twenty-four hours. Then, of course—' he gave a wave of his hand '—someone else is staying in the place I was supposed to be renting.'

She blinked. 'Have they given you a refund?'

He jerked a little. The thought had clearly not crossed his mind. 'I haven't even asked,' he admitted. 'I was just so wound up at the time and realised I had to get to the hospital. The agency weren't exactly helpful. Couldn't even promise they'd find me alternative accommodation. I'll get back onto them in the morning.'

She gave him a smile which she hoped

didn't show her true feelings. 'It's a bad time of year. This is when most of the international university students move in.'

Dougie groaned. 'Well. You've given me a week's trial. I promise I'll try and find somewhere to go in the next week.' He licked his lips and she tried not to focus on them, keeping her eyes on the rest of the people on the sidewalks. 'I know you feel kind of strong-armed into giving me a place to stay. And I'm sorry about that—but I am grateful. I just want a place to get my head down and get some actual sleep before my shift tomorrow. I hate the foggy feeling in my brain that comes from no sleep. You can't be like that in a NICU. I've always believed it's a place you have to be at over a hundred per cent. Nothing can be missed. Nothing overlooked. The condition of these kids can change in a gust of wind. It's so, so important that I'm on it.'

The skin on her arms prickled. There was something about the way he said those words. She could hear the commitment and passion for his job. Something she knew instantly would be unquestionable. But there was something else in there. Something she couldn't quite put her finger on.

'We're always on it.' The words came out automatically. Defensively. Even though she didn't entirely mean them to. But Dougie shot her what she read as a questioning glance—as if he wasn't quite convinced by what she said. And that *did* make her defensive. She worked in what she considered one of the best NICUs in the country. Dougie was lucky to have got a position there.

'I just need a chance to shake off the jet-lag,' he said. But there was something in his tone she didn't like. She gestured towards the pizza place to their left and tried not to bristle as he automatically held the door open for her. Her grandmother would have called it good old-fashioned manners. But her feminist side wanted to tell him she could hold open her own doors. It didn't help that two servers behind the counter shot each other a completely readable glance. *Hot.* Alice instantly felt their eyes on her, the split-second head-to-toe glance, wondering what Alice had, to have captured the almost movie star in their midst.

As if she were in some kind of B-movie, things happened exactly the way she could have predicted. She was instantly ignored. One of the servers leaned across the counter to talk to Dougie and ask him for his order, then her eyes widened at the accent and both started talking at once. 'Are you from Scotland? Ireland? We love your accent! Say something again? It's fabulous. It's just like Gerard Butler, or James McAvoy.'

Alice moved up to the counter alongside him. She was wearing jeans and a red top. She might not look like a female movie star, but she knew she could scrub up just as well as any of these girls. 'I had you more as a Billy Connolly myself,' she said quietly, referring to the Scottish, much older, comedian.

Dougie let out a laugh, and while he did that she quickly gave her order. It was the first time she'd seen him look truly relaxed. And she hated the way that made her stomach clench with an unwelcome wave of attraction. That was the last thing she needed at work. Her sister might have been happy to date a guy from work and get in a relationship with him, but Alice had always thought that far too messy. She preferred to keep her dating habits well away from the work place.

He gave a nod in agreement with her words. 'I think my friends back home might agree. But you do me too much credit. Nowhere near as talented as him. He's a legend.'

'Well, hopefully, you have an equal level of skill in your own specialty. Because that's where they're needed. Our hospital is renowned for having one of the best NICUs in the country. We need staff who can keep up.'

There. She'd drawn a line in the sand. Maybe this guy was just pushing all the wrong buttons. Maybe it was because she did feel things had kind of slipped out of her control and he'd been foisted on her by her sister without any real discussion. Or maybe she was just feeling conflicted by the fact she might find him a little attractive.

Whatever it was, there was something about Douglas MacLachlan she couldn't quite put her finger on. He wasn't exactly saying anything wrong out loud. But she felt as if there was a deeper meaning behind some of his words. An implication. And she wanted to put her cards completely on the table.

Dougie was leaning on the counter now and he turned back towards her. It was the first time she'd really got a proper look at those bright blue eyes of his. His eyebrows were raised. 'Oh, I think I can keep up. I just like to make sure everything is happening the way it should.'

'And why wouldn't it?' She couldn't help the snappy tone. 'Our NICU functioned well before you got here, and it will function just as well after you leave.'

Maybe it was a bit much. The girls behind

the counter took a step back and exchanged glances again—thoughts of flirtation clearly vanishing. Alice frowned, but stood her ground. She'd said it now, and had no plans to back down.

'Safety first, Nurse Greene,' he said in a low voice. 'We have the most vulnerable patients on the planet and it's up to us to protect them.'

Alice swallowed, feeling the steam rapidly rising from her toes all the way up to her ears. She was pretty sure her face was turning the same colour as her shirt. This guy was clearly going to drive her crazy. She had to work with him. But that didn't mean she had to live with him.

Then he gave her a killer smile. But it didn't quite reach his eyes. It was almost as if he'd remembered he was still slightly at her mercy and it wouldn't do to make her mad before he'd finally got the night's sleep that he craved.

She bit her bottom lip. He'd told her a few times he was tired. She'd already seen him a bit cranky earlier today when he hadn't eaten. Alice took a breath and tried to imagine how she might feel in the same circumstances.

Overlong journey. No proper food. Having

to turn up at new workplace, dragging her cases behind her, with no real place to stay that night, and completing a shift at work.

Okay. Maybe it was time to give him just the tiniest bit of leeway. But this was a one-off.

'Why did you come to Washington?' she asked. His eyes flashed and that was when she knew she'd hit a nerve with what she thought was a fairly benign question.

'Wanted a change.' The words seemed forced.

'You were in London somewhere, weren't you?'

'St Gabriel's.' The words were still tight. It was clear this was something he didn't want to discuss but all of Alice's spider senses were tingling. She was curious. She wanted to push. This guy had made a sideways comment about processes being in place.

Just at that moment her phone started to buzz. She pulled it from her pocket. It was an unknown number. 'Hello?'

There was a crackle and feedback at the end of the line. Then...nothing.

Strange. She gave a shrug and put it back in her pocket. One of the girls behind the counter pushed forward two pizza boxes. 'That's your order.'

Dougie reached out and took them both before she had a chance. 'Thanks,' he said, turning around and holding open the door for her—again.

Alice followed him outside and they started back along the street. The smell from the pizza boxes drifted towards her and her stomach growled loudly.

'Hey,' he said over his shoulder, 'you're starting to sound like me.'

She gave a weak smile. 'Maybe. But it's been a long day. I don't have much drinks-wise back at the house. Coffee, some soda, maybe a beer?'

Dougie groaned. 'A beer. A beer would be brilliant.' He closed his eyes, even though they were walking along the street. 'Now, if you had a sports channel that would make the world complete.'

'Ah,' she said, trying to hide the smile on her face. 'I think you'll find I have a cable-wide ban on sports.'

His eyes widened and he turned to her in surprise. 'Really?'

'Absolutely. My house, my rules. Movies or music.'

'That was it.' A huge grin spread across

his face. 'I've got it. The ringtone on your phone. It's an oldie.'

She gave him a curious glance. 'It is,' was all she was prepared to give away.

'But I recognised it from a film.'

Her eyebrow arched. 'Really? What film? And be careful here, if you guess wrong you lose.'

'What do I lose?'

'Our NICU game. It's our latest fun. Pick a ringtone from an old movie and you get to keep it until someone guesses correctly.' She patted her pocket. 'I'm kind of fond of this one, so I hope you're about to guess wrong.' She held up her finger. 'And you only get one guess a day. So choose wisely.'

'Maybe I'll save my guess. Give you time to play the tune a bit longer.'

She nodded slowly. 'Interesting tactic. But if you want to guess, know that you have to join the game from that point on. There's no free guesses here. You're either in or you're out.'

She couldn't pretend she wasn't still curious about what had annoyed him earlier. But it seemed to have passed just as quickly as she'd noticed it. When he wanted to be, Dougie MacLachlan could be almost charming.

'Oh, I'm in,' he said without a second's hesitation.

'That was confident. Are you an eighties fan?'

'Seventies, eighties, nineties, and everything else.' He breathed deeply, clearly inhaling the pizza. 'This could be dangerous territory when we get back. If I can't watch some sports, I can challenge you to a movie marathon.'

'You think?'

'Absolutely.'

They'd reached the townhouse again and she pulled out her keys. It only took a few minutes to rearrange the pizza boxes on the small table in the main room in front of the TV. Alice grabbed the two solitary beers that she had in the bottom of the fridge and opened them, carrying them through and lifting the remote control. She flicked the television on and selected a streaming service, where she flicked through some older movies.

'Action, sci-fi, cute, romance...' she started.

'I'd love to go for sci-fi, but let's have something out of season.'

'You want a Christmas movie?'

He shook his head and lifted a finger. 'No,

but the ultimate Christmas movie is *Die Hard* and we're not going to fight about that.'

She burst out laughing as she lifted a slice of pizza. 'So what did you have in mind? Something for summer—*Jaws*?'

'No, let's go witches. A bit of *Hocus Pocus*.'

She looked at him in surprise and gave a slow nod. 'Interesting choice.'

'Surprised?'

Intrigued, she wanted to say, but kept it to herself. She found the movie and started playing it, but after a few slices of pizza and half a bottle of beer she could literally see Dougie wilting beside her.

'You should go on up to bed.'

He sighed and nodded. 'You're right. I'm too tired. Sorry, but I need to make sure I feel fine for tomorrow.' He glanced at his watch. It was barely ten o'clock. 'You're twelve hours tomorrow. Maybe you should turn in too.'

And just as she'd thought Dougie MacLachlan might actually be bearable, he'd annoyed her again. She stood up abruptly, lifting the pizza boxes.

'You worry about you, and let me worry about me,' she said smartly.

He looked for a second as if he might answer her back, and she was ready for him.

But Dougie gave a nod and headed to the stairs. ''Night,' was the only word he uttered as he went.

And, just like that, Alice Greene knew this was never going to work out.

CHAPTER THREE

DOUGIE WAS FINALLY well rested and feeling wide awake. Alice had been a little off with him last night and things had been a bit awkward on the way to work. But she'd talked him through the subway lines and stops, where to get a ticket that lasted all day or week, and given him a few safety tips.

The route seemed straightforward and he did wonder if he might jog into work and shower and change once there. But that could all be worked out later.

There were fifty-two beds in this state-of-the-art Level IV NICU, with a whole host of specialists and staff on duty at any one time. Dougie was part of a rota of twenty-eight doctors. There was more than three times that number of nursing staff. And a whole load of other specialist paediatric staff—respiratory therapists, pharmacists—who all swiped in and out of the unit throughout the day.

Infection control measures were good—
they had to be when the footfall could mean
numerous staff required to deliver care to the
multiple babies. The noise level was a low
persistent hum of quiet conversations and ma-
chines working. It was rare to hear anything
loud in this environment. All staff were conscious of protecting their vulnerable patients.

Dougie had been given a brief on the patients he was responsible for and was making
his way around the unit, introducing himself
to each of the parents and chatting through
how their baby or babies were doing. He realised quite quickly that two of his patients,
Ruby and Ryan, born at twenty-four weeks,
were also being cared for by Alice. She was
dressed today in pale blue scrubs with teddy
bears on them.

He took one glance at the young mum sitting beside the incubators and pulled up a
chair. 'Hi, Angie, I'm Dougie MacLachlan.
I'm a new neonatologist and will be helping
to care for Ruby and Ryan.'

'How long have you been a neonatologist?'
came the quick answer. Straight to the point.
He could understand that.

'Six years.'

She let out a sigh. He knew immediately
it was relief. Most hospitals like this were

teaching hospitals. Parents could often meet a whole host of people involved in the care of their baby, and whilst no one liked to object to people learning, parents in NICU were understandably anxious.

'Where are you from?'

'Scotland, but I last worked in London in a NICU there.'

Alice moved over, giving him a nod, and started talking in a low but bright tone to Ruby as she tended to her.

'How do you feel Ruby and Ryan are doing?'

He always started like this. He'd learned it was really important to ascertain what parents understood about their babies, and to get some insight into how they were feeling about things.

Angie blinked back unshed tears. He'd checked her notes and could see that there was no mention of a father and very little family support whilst she'd been in NICU with her babies. 'Ryan is sickest,' she said quickly. 'They put a feeding tube in but he just doesn't seem to have any energy at all. His skin is peeling and I hardly even want to touch him in case I'm hurting him.'

Dougie looked up and Alice's wide brown eyes met his. 'We've talked about this, Angie,' she said reassuringly. 'You know that we want you to have as much contact with Ryan as is safe. His breathing, temperature and blood pressure are still being monitored. As soon as we're sure it will be safe, you'll be able to hold him for yourself for longer times.'

Angie blinked and turned away. 'Is there anyone else we can invite to come into the unit to support you?' Dougie asked.

'No.' It was a definite one-word answer.

Dougie persisted. He sat patiently with Angie and talked her through first Ryan's care, and then Ruby's. Alice was working on both babies as they spoke, and every now and then broke in gently to ask Angie if she wanted to assist with something.

Angie was reluctant, but one glance between him and Alice let him know they were in agreement—this was fear, nothing else.

When it reached a certain time, Alice glanced at the clock on the wall. 'Angie, I'm going to take a break. Would you like to come down to the canteen with me and get something to eat?'

Angie shook her head immediately.

'Dr MacLachlan will stay with the babies,' said Alice. He had a whole host of other things to do, but was quick to offer reassurance.

'I'm happy to,' he said. Anything to try and persuade this frail young woman to get something to eat.

But Angie was determined. 'No, I'm fine.'

Alice gave her a wide smile. 'Well, I'll pick you up something when I'm down there.' She didn't wait for Angie to give her a reply. Just finished up what she was doing, washed her hands and recorded a few things in the electronic record.

Dougie finished a few things himself then followed her down to the canteen since Angie clearly wasn't going to move.

She glanced over her shoulder in surprise when he called her name. Then watched with a smile on her face as he picked up some bacon and made some toast. 'Very British,' she said. 'The bagel and cream cheese didn't work out for you?'

'I was very grateful,' he said carefully as he pressed a button on the coffee machine. 'Can we talk about Angie?'

Alice moved her tray along and added some fruit and yoghurt. 'Sure,' she said as they paid and headed over to a table.

She was interested that he'd followed her down to the canteen to have this conversation.

'What are your thoughts?' he asked.

'Actually,' Alice said carefully, 'I'd like to know what your thoughts are. Your first impressions.'

'Is this a test?'

'You're a new doctor. I like to see how my new colleagues operate.'

He sat back in his chair, his blue eyes watching her carefully. After a thoughtful silence he gave a nod, leaning back and taking a bite of his bacon sandwich. 'She's very young, and very pale. I only have the babies' notes, but I'd be interested to know if she's anaemic, and if she's eating.'

Alice gave a slow nod but didn't say anything.

'I'm also worried about the lack of support. Have you got any idea of her family background? Twins are hard for any mum. But for a new mum, and a young mum, on her own? Particularly now she's had a premature delivery, and we're not quite sure as yet what outcomes these children are going to have, I have a whole host of worries for this family.'

Alice licked her lips. 'Anything else?'

Dougie gave a half smile. 'I guess I'm not quite meeting your standards. But I'm not finished. Ruby seems to be doing well. Ryan is not so good. I'd like to do some more tests on him. His oxygen sats fluctuate, and he gives the appearance of a baby who is dehydrated, even though our fluid charts don't seem to support that. But I've to go with what I see. I'm checking his bloods again when I go back.' He bit his bottom lip, clearly thinking about something else. 'Do you think there's any chance that Angie has an eating disorder? She's hidden under mounds of clothes, so it's hard to tell. Her arms and face are thin. Is there a midwife coming to see her, doing checks? If there is, I'd like to have a chat with her.'

Alice sat back in her seat and looked at him with interest. He'd barely had a chance to read the notes and get to know Angie and her children, but he seemed to already be thinking widely about the situation. She was interested in him telling her that even though fluid charts were telling him Ryan was adequately hydrated, he was more concerned by what he was observing.

The words about Angie were interesting too. Alice had noticed the fact she wasn't really eating much, and had just put it down to her being overwhelmed by her current situation. But it could be something else. And she was glad he'd mentioned it—even if it ended up being something they could rule out.

'Have I passed your test yet?' His eyes had a wicked gleam in them.

She stirred her fruit into her yoghurt. 'Maybe. But I like to take my time over a new colleague before I make any judgement.'

Her phone sounded in her pocket and he laughed. 'Okay, I've definitely won. It's Huey Lewis and the News and it's from *Back to the Future*. Good pick, by the way.'

She gave a sorry nod. 'I was hoping to keep this one for a bit longer. But I guess it's time to find something else. Are you joining in?'

He pulled his own phone from his pocket and pressed a button. A ringtone started and she wrinkled her brow, concentrating. The tune was definitely familiar, but the name of the movie wasn't jumping out at her.

'I've got you.' He smiled. 'That's going to annoy you all day now, isn't it?'

The edges of her mouth hinted at a smile. 'You have no idea.'

'You need to play to win,' he said. 'Don't pick the obvious tracks. Don't pick the one song that was the statement for the film. Pick something else. Something from a key scene. Something that comes on the radio and everyone looks at each other and says—what's that from again?'

Alice narrowed her gaze. This guy was

toying with her—deliberately trying to annoy her. But there was a hint of something else. Was he flirting with her? She hadn't even found out if he had any kind of attachment back home. Her stomach gave a little clench. Did she actually want to know?

She tapped her fingers on the table. 'Are you trying to tell me how to play my own game?'

He leaned back a bit further, amusement written all over his face. 'Oh, it's *your* game, is it?'

She could take this. She folded her arms and looked him straight in the eye. 'Yes, it's my game, and I intend to win.' Something sparked in her brain. 'I'm going to put a chart up in the office in NICU. We'll see who can get the most points.'

'Are you going to give me credit for my first point?'

'I get the sense of someone playing to win.'

'Of course. Otherwise, what's the point?'

Just at that, his phone rang for real and both of them jumped and started laughing. Dougie answered quickly. 'Douglas MacLachlan?'

She watched as he nodded and gave short answers. It was clear this was not a call he was happy with. Next came the questions. 'And when will that be? Why can't it be sooner? How much availability? No, that's totally unsuitable. I'm a doctor. I don't have a car. I need to be able to use public transport to get to the hospital.'

The conversation seemed to be going from bad to worse. Deep furrows appeared across his brow and his jaw and mouth were tight. His free hand clenched into a fist and she could see he was starting to get angry. She could partly hear some of the conversation at the other end. Whoever it was clearly didn't have a care in the world, and certainly didn't care that they'd double-booked an apartment and left a doctor without somewhere to stay. Dougie was understandably getting more and more wound up, then suddenly, in a moment that surprised nobody more than Alice herself, she reached over and touched his hand, giving a gentle shake of her head. 'Not worth it,' she mouthed.

She tried to ignore the immediate sensations shooting up her arm as her skin came into contact with his. It was nothing. Nothing at all. But it didn't *feel* like nothing. His gaze met hers and she wondered if he felt it too.

She could see the tension across all his muscle groups, but after a few moments he gave her a small nod and relaxed, asking for some further feedback and ending the call.

He stayed silent for a few moments, eyes fixed on his phone lying on the table. Alice swallowed uncomfortably. She really couldn't get a handle on this guy at all. Sometimes she wanted to give him a sympathy hug, other times he annoyed every cell in her body. Then there was the touch thing that she was currently keeping in the 'ignore' box.

He leaned his head on one hand. 'They've found me a place thirty kilometres away.'

'*What?*'

'Oh, good. So I'm not completely unreasonable then?'

She shook her head. 'No, you're not. They can't expect you to travel that distance when you've no transport and have to rely on public transport. You could get called into the hospital in the middle of the night.'

'Yeah, they don't care about that.' He shook his head and stowed his phone back in his pocket. 'I'll see if they get back to me later.' He pushed his chair back. 'We'd better get back to the unit.'

She picked up the remains of her breakfast and dumped it in the trash, then grabbed another candy bar and coffee for Angie. 'It's not healthy eating at all,' she said. 'But it's the only thing I've seen her eat whilst on the unit. So I'm going to get her some while we have a think about what you said earlier.' As they walked back along the corridor she gave him a sideways glance. 'And, just so you know, you're still on a trial period at my house. I might let you stay—particularly if you do any of the baking you promised.'

He held open the door for her. 'Baking bribery.' He gave a contemplative nod. 'It might be the skill I'll have to use.'

She wagged her finger at him. 'And as for that ringtone. It's giving me ear worm. It keeps playing in my head.'

He tapped his nose. 'Nope. Not giving that one up. You have to play fair and square. And no internet browsing.' He pointed to her head, his finger accidentally brushing a few stray hairs at the side of her brow. 'It has to come from the deep recesses of your brain. Otherwise, it doesn't count.'

'Spoilsport,' she said as she turned and walked over to the sink to wash her hands.

Penny appeared instantly at her elbow. 'You two making friends? That looked cosy.' She had a wide smile on her face, but that only put Alice on edge.

'We're not all playing the romance game. It was a simple conversation. Nothing more, nothing less. He actually annoys me at times.'

Penny gave her a look. 'Benedict used to annoy me at times too,' she said in a tone only a sister could use, before she disappeared across the unit again.

Alice sighed. Dougie had sat back down next to Angie and was talking to her again. She was glad he was taking an interest in their patient. Some neonatologists appeared to focus only on the babies, but Alice appreciated those who spent equal amounts of time with the parents. The psychological aspects of being a parent to an early and sometimes sick baby had only really been understood well in the last few years.

It wasn't unusual for the unit to still get calls from parents whose children had been patients a few years earlier. Even though staff turnover could be high, there were some, like Alice, who had worked here for more than a few years, and there was always someone who would be available to chat with a worried parent.

She watched for a few moments. She still wasn't sure about this guy. From here, as he talked sincerely and then made a few jokes with Angie, he looked like the perfect handsome guy, with a killer accent. But there was something else there. Something else beneath the surface. And she just didn't know what it was.

But Alice, being Alice, would have to find out.

For the first half of the next week, Dougie actually felt quite comfortable finding his feet in the unit. It was hard to keep track of all the staff. In a unit as big as this, he did his best to remember the names of everyone he came into contact with. Angie was still proving to be a little bit of a mystery. He didn't want to put the young mum under any kind of pressure, and he hadn't freely discussed his concerns with any other staff, but he and Alice were doing their best to build a rapport with her and allay her concerns.

He'd also spent a bit of time checking processes within the unit. The fact was, he just couldn't help it. His experience in the last unit in London had scarred him for life, he feared. One newly appointed member of staff, who at first had seemed friendly and well-adjusted, had proved to be much more dangerous. At first, it had just been a few odd words here and there. A few excuses about things not done quite as they should be. Nothing had been risky…nothing had caused any adverse events. Other staff had mentioned, or casually corrected her on a few occasions. But Kayla had a big personality. She was a people person, exceedingly friendly. Inviting people to join her for drinks or dinner. Patients loved her. A bit of a whirlwind, but so nice. And that was it. That was the downfall that Dougie had been swept into, along with others.

There had even been a date that hadn't amounted to anything, even though Kayla had been keen to take things further. And so had Dougie, but something had stopped him. And to this day he didn't know what.

Something had just seemed amiss. Even though he hadn't wanted to, he'd started to watch. He'd mentioned to the charge nurse in the unit—the most switched-on person he'd ever met—a few potential mistakes. She'd been annoyed at first, and talked to him about the seriousness of raising competency issues. But Dougie had been quietly insistent, not making a fuss but ensuring his concerns were noted.

And that was when everything had started to unravel. Staff had talked to each other. Dougie had started to notice quietened voices and suspicious glances towards him—not Kayla. Then someone else had started in a neighbouring ward, someone who'd worked at the same hospital as Kayla before, and she'd made a few comments that resulted in Dougie and the charge nurse taking advice from HR colleagues. When they'd all dug a little deeper it appeared that Kayla had moved quickly from place to place. A few calls had been made to her previous workplaces. Yes, there had been a few incidents. There had been suspicions, but nothing had been proven.

His gut had been telling him something that he had absolutely no proof of.

Finally, on a night he'd never forget, he'd watched her draw up some medicine and stopped her before she'd left the treatment room. The charge nurse was by his side. Although the prescription was correct, the medicine had been wrongly constituted; the incorrect dose was in the syringe. It was a mistake that other people might have made in the past. The dose got absolutely nowhere near the patient it was intended for. But Kayla had been put on supervised practice only and left some time later—entirely her own decision—letting everyone know that Dougie had wrongly accused her of intentional malpractice all because she'd refused to go on a second date with him.

None of this had been true. But he'd noticed that laughter had died around him, and invitations to nights out and get-togethers had dwindled.

When he'd heard that Kayla had been charged nine months later with attempted murder while working somewhere else he'd blamed himself. There had been no trace of where she'd gone; she'd not asked for any references when she'd left. The charge nurse at his NICU had put in an alert to the governing nurse body.

The truth had only been discovered when police came to the unit, asking for statements from staff who'd previously worked with her.

Dougie had been devastated. He should have trusted his gut, but those around him had questioned his motives. He became a person he'd never wanted to be—one who watched everyone around him constantly.

It was a sad fact of life that errors happened every day in hospitals and other care settings. Most were never intentional, and some a result of procedures not being followed, information not updated or pure human error. But Dougie had felt himself becoming obsessed.

It probably didn't help that most of the staff who still worked with him all blamed themselves too for not listening to his initial concerns, and for doubting him. But when he'd started to double-check everything that people were doing, their patience eventually grew thin.

The Head of Department had sat him down and told him, even though he was a wonderful doctor, it was time for a change of scene. He was becoming too wrapped up in what had happened before and how he could prevent it ever happening again that people were spending their lives tiptoeing around him.

He knew that; he could sense it. And when his mentor had told him about the job in Washington Dougie had known it was the right move to make. A new country. New faces. New patients. And no one who would know his past experience.

He was trying his best not to let his past affect him, but he knew that it always would. He could never be comfortable working anywhere until he knew there were protocols and safety checks in place that met the standards in his head. And it wasn't just his work that had been affected; it was his personal life too. He'd been on a date with Kayla. Just one.

But now he was questioning his judgement. He'd allowed himself to be carried along with her warm and friendly manner. It didn't matter that it had only been one date. It had left Kayla with the ammunition to claim that Dougie's questions about her practice were those of a scorned partner. If he'd never gone on that date, that would never have happened. He felt duped. Dating had definitely taken a back seat ever since.

His housing situation had not been resolved in any way, shape or form. To be honest, he'd thought that the rental company might have taken more responsibility for their mistake. He'd been kidding himself. The fact of the matter was they were indifferent and un-apologetic. In their view, they'd made a half-hearted attempt to find alternative ac-commodation, which was completely unsuit-able, and Dougie had turned it down, so they were done.

He hadn't quite mentioned this to Alice yet. But as he went from market place to small store, he knew it was time to try and win favour with his housemate. Baking utensils were hard to come by in the heart of Wash-ington DC. But, thanks to some hints from other work colleagues, he finally had what he needed.

Alice had told him she was going shopping after work, so by the time she got home he'd planned for everything to be ready.

Ovens could be unpredictable for a baker. He'd learned this early on in life. Some ran hotter than the dial, some colder, affecting the length of stay in the oven, and the potential for soggy bottoms or dry overcooked bases or sponges.

Dougie would have preferred a few trial runs, but there just hadn't been time. Red velvet muffins and, her apparent favourite, banana loaf were already cooling on the wire rack under a tea towel. He was currently waiting for the sponges of a chocolate fudge cake to finish in the oven.

The noise of the door opening made him turn around. 'What is that smell?' came the immediate question.

Alice appeared a few moments later in jeans and a yellow top, swinging a bag in her hand. She didn't wait, just moved across the floor and sat at the kitchen table.

'You've finally come good on your early promises,' she said. 'I was beginning to think you'd just told me you could bake to try and get a bed for the night.'

'Might have been true,' he admitted.

She stood up and moved to check the trash can. 'Just making sure there are no bakery store cartons.'

'What a suspicious mind,' he said as he shook his head.

She grinned. 'Might have done it myself before.'

'Sneaky.'

'Maybe.' Her phone sounded and as she pulled it from her pocket he turned the vaguely familiar-sounding tune over in his mind. But the expression on her face made him pause.

'What's wrong?'

She pulled a face and kept her eyes on the screen before swiping it away. 'Nothing. Just some weird messages.'

'Why would you be getting weird messages?'

She sighed and ran her fingers through her hair as he sat down opposite her, checking the timer on his own phone. 'It's just via a dating app that I use sometimes. Guess I'm attracting the wrong type.'

'You use a dating app?' He couldn't help how surprised he sounded.

He could see her growing instantly defensive. 'What's wrong with a dating app? It's how the modern world works.'

He held up his hands. 'Nothing. Nothing at all. I guess I just thought a girl like you wouldn't need a dating app.'

'A girl like me? What does that mean?'

Dougie instantly knew that he'd unwittingly dug a hole for himself that he was unlikely to climb out of. 'I mean you're good-looking and you're smart.'

'Like the rest of the world,' she said quickly. 'Good-looking, smart and time-limited. I don't want to spend my life in bars in the random hope of maybe meeting someone. I work long hours. I'm covering for absent colleagues right now. If I want to go on a date— I want to go on a date. Apps work for me. I look for someone who might like some of the same things I do—not too many, though. That could be boring.'

Dougie relaxed a little but reached behind him and grabbed the cooling racks, bringing them to the table and unveiling the red velvet cupcakes and banana loaf.

She inhaled deeply and sighed.

'So, you're not looking for a perfect match then?' he asked.

She shook her head as he grabbed some plates and a knife. 'I guess a perfect match has always sounded a little boring to me.'

He smiled and nodded as he checked through the glass oven door. Another few minutes. 'So, variety is the spice of life?'

She groaned. 'That old one. It always sounds a bit off, doesn't it? What's in the oven?'

She was eyeing the cakes in front of her

with a knife in one hand. 'Chocolate sponges,' he said, 'for a chocolate fudge cake. I still have to make the filling and the topping, but they have to cool first. Otherwise, it just ends up a splodgy melted mess.'

She laughed and started cutting a slice of the banana loaf. 'Guess I'll start here then. Any butter?'

Dougie pulled back. 'Whoa. You're going to desecrate my banana loaf with butter?'

'I know how I like it,' she said as she met his gaze. There was an odd moment of silence. Dougie had to remind himself they were talking about cake. He swung his legs around as he laughed, opening the refrigerator and pulling out butter and two beers.

'You shopped?' she said, accepting both the beer and the butter.

'I even bought chicken,' he said. 'Something that might actually be a dinner.'

'This isn't dinner?' She looked up from where she was slathering butter on his banana loaf.

'You know you're ruining it, don't you?'

Her phone sounded again and she frowned.

The Breakfast Club,' he said instantly, recognising the tune and the movie it came from. 'That one was kind of wasted on me. Simple

Minds—Scottish band—always going to recognise them.'

'Took you two listens,' she murmured, her head still over her phone.

'Got a better offer?' He was talking about the ringtone, but realised his words might be misconstrued when she was clearly checking out a message on her dating app.

Even though her hair was partly covering her face, he could see her jaw tighten. With a swish of her fingers the app was deleted. She stood up and disappeared for a few seconds. From the noises he could hear, she was checking the front door.

'Everything okay?' The words came out automatically even though it was clear that everything wasn't okay.

She lifted her head as she climbed up the two steps into the kitchen and shook back her hair. Her cheeks were slightly flushed. There was false bravado on her face and that made his stomach twist in a protective way he didn't expect.

'Fine.' It was one word. But it had a tiny waver to it. 'Plenty more dating apps to use.'

His brain switched gear. 'Anything you need to tell me?' There was much more to this story. But he wasn't sure he had any right to pry. He'd known Alice Greene for less than a week.

She pressed her lips together for a few moments. It was clear she was mulling things over. Dougie knew when to be quiet.

He couldn't really read her yet. If she needed to talk, he could do that. If she needed to be left alone, he could do that too. If she needed distraction, he was the king of that. But sitting here waiting was killing him.

And he couldn't really understand why.

She took a bite of the banana loaf and then a swig from her beer bottle, setting it down on the table firmly.

'Okay,' she said. 'You can stay.'

'What?' It seemed to come out of nowhere. And he was completely aware she'd ignored his earlier question.

She held out one hand. 'You seem relatively clean. You do your own laundry. You don't leave things lying around. I haven't heard you snoring. You buy groceries—and beer. And...you can bake. You can stay.'

It was the best news he'd heard all week.

But he tilted his head to one side. 'I seem *relatively* clean?'

The edges of her lips turned upwards. 'I haven't got that close. And I don't intend to.'

Those final words were probably a bit of

an insult that if he'd had a few more beers he might have teased her over. But Dougie knew this wasn't the time.

'Okay. That's great. Thanks. Although I can't promise not to annoy you sometimes, I can at least promise to try not to annoy you. And to remain relatively clean.' He took a pointed swig from his own beer bottle.

'The banana loaf is good,' she conceded as she lifted one of the cupcakes, peeled off the foil wrapper and cut the cake in half.

As she examined the rich red sponge she kept talking. 'I figure since you're already here and haven't found someplace else, it makes much more sense if we just keep this arrangement going. I don't know anyone else looking for somewhere to rent, and I'd have to advertise and interview people I don't know.' She wrinkled her nose. 'Not really sure I'm up for that right now.' Her brown eyes met his. 'So far, you seem pretty safe.'

And that was it. She probably didn't even realise that she'd said it. But Dougie had always been able to pick up on unconscious cues. It was part of what made him a good doctor.

Safety was important to Alice Greene right now. And something about her latest interaction with the dating app had made her feel unsafe.

Dougie didn't like that. He didn't like it at all. But he also knew it wasn't his business or place to say anything.

His eyes focused on the digital numbers on his own phone and he jumped up. 'Darn it!' He pulled the oven door down and grabbed for the nearby oven mitt, pulling the chocolate sponges from the heat.

'Did you forget about them?'

He grimaced. 'Momentarily distracted.'

She moved over next to him and leaned over the three sponges. Her arm brushed against his. He knew it was inadvertent but something stopped him from stepping away. Her light floral scent drifted around him, mixed in with the chocolate sponges.

'They aren't burnt,' she said, still staring at them.

He pressed one with a fingertip. It didn't bounce back quite as much as it should have. 'Still a bit overdone.'

She turned around, tilting her chin up to face him. 'But you're going to make that fudge sauce. Who'll notice if the sponges are a bit dry?' This was the closest they had ever been. She suited the yellow shirt. It reflected off her tanned skin and dark hair and eyes. She had a bit of eyeliner on, smudged around her lower lids. And that had to be mascara, because no ordinary person could have lashes that long and perfectly separated. As for her lips?

Dougie blinked. He couldn't remember the last time he'd thought about a woman in detail like this. She was still looking up at him and he grinned. 'I vote that tonight we leave the chicken in the fridge and eat three slightly dry sponges, smothered in chocolate fudge sauce.'

She put her hand to her chest, drawing his eyes now to the skin at the bottom of her throat and the glimpse where two buttons hadn't been fastened. 'It's a sacrifice I think I can make. We could even pick an eighties movie to watch while we do it.'

He licked his lips. His words were a bit hoarser than he liked. 'You're going to sacrifice yourself by eating my cake?'

She raised her eyebrows. 'Someone's gotta do it. You know, take one for the team.'

She laughed, finally stepping back and breaking the weird vibe that had settled around them.

He pulled a saucepan from a drawer and said over his shoulder, 'You have to pick an eighties film we've already used. Would hate to think you were about to try and cheat and find out where my ringtone comes from.'

She shot him a glare. 'It's driving me nuts!'

'Then things are working out perfectly. Hand me over the cooling tray. I have to tip these sponges out.'

She did it, with one hand on her hip. 'It'll have to be *Back to the Future* then. I'm in the mood for some time travel.'

'Whatever you like,' he agreed, wondering what on earth he was getting himself into.

Alice had pulled off her jeans and found some yoga pants. She realised the mistake of not changing her favourite yellow shirt the second Dougie handed her the bowl filled with chocolate sponge and an enormous helping of chocolate fudge sauce. It was still warm and smelt divine. She looked down at the shirt, knowing she could kiss it goodbye with one spilled drop. 'Give me a sec.'

She ran up the stairs, unfastening the shirt as she went, then grabbing an oversized grey T-shirt instead. When she got back down, Dougie had the TV paused at the credits for the movie.

She settled herself cross-legged on the floor between the sofa and the coffee table that held her bowl of cake.

'That can't be comfy,' came the thick Scottish accent.

She waved her spoon as she dived in. 'What won't be comfy is you—if you drop that sauce on my cream sofa. The beauty of a wooden floor is that everything wipes clean.'

Two seconds later he thumped down next to her as he hit play on the remote. She laughed as he tried, and failed, to fold his much longer legs up into the space between the sofa and table. Eventually he gave a sigh and pushed the table a bit further forward.

There was something about being around Douglas MacLachlan. Maybe it was just his size. His over-six-foot frame and his broad shoulders. Maybe it was just the association with the accent—in every movie she'd ever seen, you didn't mess with a Scotsman.

But right now she felt safe around Dougie.

That last message via the app had been unsettling. The mention of her yellow shirt had freaked her out completely. It wasn't something she was going to tell him—that some random guy who'd liked her via a dating app had sent a few pointed messages in the last few days. But it unnerved her.

So when she'd got home to the smell of home baking, tasted it and then contemplated having to advertise for a roommate, she knew she had to invite Dougie to stay. If he'd told her the rental agency had sorted things out, she might have cried. The thought of even being alone in this place made her distinctly uncomfortable.

Alice Greene was a girl who'd always been comfortable in her own skin. But her bad experience when Penny was in Ohio had unsettled her, and now tonight's message had thrown her.

Pretty shirt. Yellow. Like a sunflower.

It was hardly a threatening message. But that was exactly how it felt. As if someone was watching her. Which made her feel immensely glad to have someone like Dougie around. She didn't know him well at all. But her instincts about him were good.

There was a strong likelihood he might annoy her at work, but as long as she felt safe having him around then she was glad he was here.

Trouble was, having a man with an accent like his, along with leading guy looks, *and* the ability to make chocolate fudge sauce like this—was surely asking for trouble.

For a second when she'd looked up at him in the kitchen, one glimpse of those big blue eyes had swept all the panic she'd felt earlier away. Just the sensation of having him close made her feel protected. Which was ridiculous, and she knew it. Particularly when her eyes had been distracted by those lips...

She was being stupid now. But as she leaned back against the sofa to watch the opening credits of one of her favourite movies, while enjoying all the sensations of the rich cake, she felt strangely happy.

If Penny could see this scene right now she would be asking a million questions. And Alice wasn't sure she could answer any one of them. Best to say nothing. Best to keep things to herself.

Dougie turned his phone around so she could see it. 'Took a selfie outside the White House today.' He looked proud of himself. 'Where else can I go?'

'Wait until you have a few days off. I'll take you to some of the best bits of Washington. There's much more here than you think.'

'Like what?'

'Abe Lincoln's summer cottage, the woods of Theodore Roosevelt Island, the National Museum of Health and Medicine has some exhibits that will make you grue, and then—' she smiled at him '—I've got a special surprise for you at the Botanic Gardens.'

Dougie blinked and looked at her cautiously.

Alice smirked. 'Let's just say it'll be a day you won't forget.'

He shifted, his shoulder brushing against hers. 'And you don't mind?'

She turned her face to him. 'Why would I? My sister is happily in love, one of my best friends is away in Spain to help her family. I have time.'

He nodded slowly. 'Well, thank you. I appreciate it. I like to find out a bit more about wherever I am staying. Plus, I definitely don't know where to shop for groceries. I know you told me some places the first night—but they're lost in a different world for me.' He nodded at the movie. 'Just call me Marty.'

'Okay, Marty.' She took another spoonful of cake. 'But my fees are in cakes.'

'I think I can manage that,' he said, smiling, and she wondered exactly what she was getting into.

CHAPTER FOUR

THERE WAS SOMETHING about a certain time of night in hospitals. It didn't matter whether staff worked in A&E, coronary care, a medical unit or a NICU. That strange hour in the dead of night—the witching hour some called it—usually between three and four a.m., was the time when staff circadian rhythms meant they were most tired, and irony meant that it was usually the time something happened.

'I hate night shift,' said Alice as she poured herself a coffee in the staffroom. 'I would do almost anything to get out of them.'

'Not really a fan myself,' admitted Dougie, 'but it's part of the job. And I usually use the night shift card if people tell me I'm crabbit.'

She smiled at him with her hand on one hip. 'Oh, no, I can't believe anyone would call you crabbit.'

He rolled his eyes. 'I know that's what some of the staff are saying. I just call things

like they are. If some people think it's crabbit I can live with that.'

She laughed and shook her head. 'I love
the way you say that word and, to be honest, there couldn't be a better description.'
She stirred her coffee and then sighed. 'But
I also like knackered. I've heard people in
here start to say it, and you've only been here
two weeks.'

Dougie took a sip of his coffee. 'I'm like
a virus. I come somewhere new, start using
all my Scottish words and, before you know
it, you're all joining in.'

'We should make you a chart,' Alice
mused. 'Like the ringtone one. You could
introduce a new word every week and see
how many people can use it.'

She was trying to ignore the zing she still
felt around him whenever they got too close.
Even though they still bickered at work sometimes—usually when he was being pedan-
tic about something—they generally got on
fine. She might even call her new roommate
a friend. And for Alice that was big.

For the last few years, she always joked
to Penny that she'd used up her quota of
friends and didn't have room for any more.
But Dougie was managing to wriggle his
way in there.

He'd been true to his word about baking. He was a better grocery shopper than she was—although Alice had been sure to split costs. But most of all it was just knowing there was another presence in the house that gave her some reassurance.

She was never going to admit that when she'd realised he was covering nights this week she'd swapped her shifts so she wouldn't be home alone.

She hadn't told a soul that she'd received another kind of strange message from a different dating app. One word. *Lavender.* Which was growing in a pot at her front door. She was tempted to call her old DC cop friend, just to ask if she was being paranoid. But instead she'd just deleted the app, and swapped shifts.

'My word for this week would be scunner. Usually used by grannies, along with the phrase "you're a wee scunner". I'll let you work out for yourself what you think that means.'

She laughed and pointed at his pocket. 'I've got it.'

'Got what?' He looked down at himself as if he didn't understand what she was saying.

'Your ringtone.'

'You have?' He leaned against the wall, looking interested.

'It's "Oh, Yeah", from *Ferris Bueller's Day Off.*'

'Took you long enough.'

Just as Alice opened her mouth to retort, something started to ping outside.

Their movements were automatic. Both put down their coffee and walked quickly to the incubator where the alarms were sounding. This was a new baby girl, Blossom. Born at twenty-five weeks to a mom with pre-eclampsia. She wasn't breathing on her own, and was already showing signs of jaundice. Right now, her dusky colour was giving cause for concern.

Alice glanced at the monitor and without a word grabbed a very thin suction tube from the wall. She manoeuvred it carefully, trying to remove the blockage from Blossom's air-way. After a few moments she shook her head and looked at Dougie. 'It has to be something else. I'm feeling resistance.'

Dougie helped reposition the tiny baby, delicately checking the airway again. 'I think her feeding tube has regurgitated. I'm going to start by taking it out.'

Alice took a deep breath. Putting feeding tubes in babies like this was hard work. Their oesophagi and tracheae were so tiny. Feeding tubes were always X-rayed once in position and prior to any feeding starting, to ensure everything was exactly where it should be. Any mistake could be disastrous.

Dougie removed the tiny tube smoothly and calmly. He then repositioned Blossom. Thankfully, her mom wasn't here right now to see the calamity. Although she had spent some time with her daughter, she was still in Maternity, with her blood pressure being monitored after an earlier seizure. Alice's eyes flitted between the monitor and Blossom, checking her chest and colour.

Although Dougie appeared entirely calm, she could see something in those blue eyes. He put his finger gently on Blossom's hand and talked in a low voice to her. Her heart was racing, and her dusky colour was starting to change a little.

A few other staff had appeared at their sides. 'What's up?' asked the first.

'Airway problems,' said Alice. 'Dougie's just removed the feeding tube. It looks as if she's settling now.'

'Who put the tube in?' Dougie asked.

No one answered. Alice imagined it was because no one knew.

'I need to see Blossom's chart. I want to

know when the tube went in. I want to see the X-ray for confirmation of position. And I want to see when the feeds started and what her observations have been since.' His voice was tense, and Alice didn't like it.

She stayed focused on the baby.

Blossom's nurse, Ron, arrived back at the side of the incubator, wide-eyed. 'What's happened?'

He'd only gone on a break fifteen minutes ago, and Alice knew exactly how he was feeling—this had happened to her too. She quickly explained and moved over to let him continue the care of his patient. He knew Blossom better than she did.

She joined Dougie, who was now at the nurses' station, checking the electronic records. The previous X-ray blinked up on the screen. Alice could see instantly the feeding tube with its guidewire still in place, showing it was exactly where it should be—in Blossom's tiny stomach.

She breathed a sigh of relief then was angry at herself. She'd known it would be. But Dougie's reaction had made her second-guess her conscientious colleagues and she hated that.

His eyes were running down her chart. 'Everything is exactly how it should be,' she said, feeling on edge.

'It wasn't when we got to her. Her naso-gastric tube had moved and was blocking her airway.'

Alice ground her teeth together. 'Look at when she was last fed. All the checks were done. The amount of visible tube is checked off. No kinking was recorded at the back of the mouth. The aspirate showed a PH below five point five. The tube was in the correct place then.'

But Dougie kept going, looking back through other notes.

After a few minutes Alice could feel herself getting mad. 'Why are you looking for something that isn't there?'

His eyes flashed as he met her gaze. 'We've just treated a baby that couldn't breathe properly. That happened in this unit, on *our* shift. It's our duty to examine every angle of this. To pick it apart, and make sure it doesn't happen again.' He'd pulled the neonatal tube feeding protocol from one of the folders. 'Maybe it's time for this to be reviewed.'

'Maybe it's time to take a breath. Sometimes tubes move. This can't be the first time this has happened to you. There might not be rhyme or reason to it.' She was trying to sound calm and rational but she was still annoyed with him. 'But it doesn't mean that anyone did something wrong.'

He turned around to face her, stopping concentrating on the chart in his lap. 'And if they did?'

'What's that supposed to mean?'

'I mean, if we'd discovered that the tube hadn't been checked, and neither had the aspirate, what then?'

Alice frowned and shifted her feet. 'None of those things happened. So why would you even ask?'

'I just wonder if you'd be willing to overlook failings in your colleagues. Pretend they didn't happen.'

That was it. Red mist descended. 'How dare you? What kind of suggestion is that? I'm a professional, as is everyone else who works in here. We are all human. And even though you might not like it, mistakes can happen. And when and if they do happen we all act appropriately. I would prioritise my patient. I would make sure they were safe. Once I was satisfied with that, I'd report the incident, let it be investigated properly and debrief with my colleagues. We have a procedure for learning incidents in the NICU—like all teaching hospitals. Don't you dare insinuate that anything would be covered up or ignored.' She was furious now. A few colleagues turned their heads and she realised that her voice must have risen.

Dougie should be embarrassed to have even asked that question, but as she stared at him she realised he wasn't embarrassed in the slightest. He was looking at her as though he still had questions.

'Do you think there's something lacking in my nursing skills?' She swung out her arm. 'Or the nursing skills of anyone is this unit? Because if you do I suggest you have a chat with Tara, our charge nurse. You might think you're a brave Scotsman, but I can tell you right now who I'd put my money on in that fight.'

His eyebrows rose and he had the cheek to look the tiniest bit amused.

'Do you think this is funny?' she demanded.

His expression changed completely and he stood up. 'No. I don't think this is funny. But what I do think is that if something goes wrong when I'm the doctor on duty then it's my job to ask questions. It's my job to look at procedures and look at everyone I'm working with.'

Those last words threw her. 'What's that supposed to mean?'

But his gaze had turned steely. 'It means that the lives of these babies are more important than any arguments between us. I can, and will, ask questions if I think they need to be asked. And I will continue to look at all the staff and all the procedures to make sure this place is as safe as it possibly can be.'

He turned and walked away, moving back over to Blossom's incubator. She could tell from the expression on Ron's face that the conversation between them was uncomfortable. Ron was a fine NICU nurse. He'd been here longer than Alice and could recite protocols in his sleep. He wouldn't mess up. She had complete faith in him.

But as she watched him answer Dougie's questions she could almost see him second-guessing himself. She wanted to go and wrap her arm around him.

Alice moved back to the four babies she was looking after. Dougie's words echoed in her head as she checked and double-checked their feeds, urine output, medicines and observations. She could do these things in her sleep, but the latest incident had made her paranoid.

That irritated her. But she wasn't sure quite what irritated most. Was it the fact that Dougie thought that someone in the unit had made a mistake and caused harm to a baby? Or was it the fact that he'd implied that staff covered for their colleagues?

As she tended to her own charges, she tried to downplay things in her head. She was tired. She hated night shift. Might she have overreacted a little? Certain things were true. Any professional should ask questions about anything that went wrong on their watch. So why was she offended by Dougie asking the questions?

As she moved to change one of her babies, she realised exactly why. Because that was the first place he'd gone. There hadn't been room to contemplate if it had just been one of those things that happened. There hadn't been a question about human error. It was as if he had just jumped to the worst possible conclusion. Someone hadn't done their job properly. Someone hadn't recorded properly. The final possibility was just too ridiculous for Alice to even consider, and she certainly hoped it hadn't featured in Dougie's mind— the fact it could have been deliberate.

Totally and utterly ridiculous.

Alice was always meticulous at work. She remembered a time as a student when one of her colleagues in an elderly ward had given the wrong patient an anticoagulant injection.

The patient had come to no harm, but the fall-out of the situation had terrified Alice about making a mistake at work.

Her colleague had been distraught. She'd got a call on the way into work to say her father had suffered a heart attack. On a normal day, she would have called in sick. But the ward had already been affected by the winter vomiting bug and several staff were already sick. If this colleague had phoned in sick too, staffing levels would have been unsafe. So the colleague had come to work, upset and distracted. She'd done the same medicine round that she'd done many times before as she knew many of the elderly patients. But beds had been swapped around as someone had deteriorated and needed to be moved to a side room. Although she'd checked the patient wrist band, it hadn't clocked in her brain and, before she knew it, she was disposing of a small syringe and realising she'd just given the medicine to the wrong patient.

There had been disciplinary action. And Alice had to give a statement as a member of staff on duty. It didn't matter she hadn't been involved in the medicine round, or that she didn't have responsibility to check the prescription or the patient.

The whole event had stayed with her for years. Even now, thinking about it filled her stomach with hollow dread. Nothing like that had happened tonight on the unit. Not even close. So why was that event now haunting her?

Enough. Alice finished her checks and moved over to talk to Ron. It was clear he was upset.

Alice didn't hesitate to give him her best smile and slip her arm around his shoulder. 'How's your girl doing?'

He sighed. 'She's fine. I just had to phone the nurse on the postnatal ward and ask her to wake up Blossom's mom in the middle of the night to tell her there had been a problem. She's distraught, even though I told her everything is fine now.'

Alice nodded. She understood. They always let patients know if there were any changes in their baby's condition, but she knew that Ron would have felt terrible doing that.

'Why don't you take another picture, and go on down and see her?' It seemed like the most reassuring thing they could do.

Ron sighed. 'I'd love to, but…' he nodded over towards Dougie '…can you imagine what Mr Braveheart might say if I suggested it?'

Alice bit the inside of her cheek, her mind made up in an instant. 'Then let me.'

She walked over to Dougie. 'Ron had to let Blossom's mom know what happened. She's understandably upset, and you'll know she's recovering from a seizure and pre-eclampsia. Stress is the last thing that woman needs.'

Dougie looked at her. For the first time, she could see some empathy on his face.

'We have to keep parents informed—' he started.

'We do,' she said, cutting him off. 'But right now we also have a duty of care to a mother as well as a baby. So either we let Ron go down, take a new picture of Blossom and talk her mother through what happened and reassure her everything's fine—' his brow was already pinched at the suggestion '—or you go down and do that. Or—' she paused '—if Ron goes, you need to sit with Blossom.'

She didn't allow there to be any choice in the matter. After tonight's event, someone would continue to sit with Blossom on a one-to-one basis for the rest of the night. Dougie looked over and she could see him trying to make up his mind.

'I'd suggest you let Ron do it, since he's already met Blossom's mom. Seems better than to send a strange doctor in the middle of the night, doesn't it?'

She was being pointed and she knew it. He could call her out. He could say as doctor on duty everything was his call. But she wanted him to understand they took a team approach here. This wasn't about him, or Ron. This was about the unit team deciding who was best to talk to mom.

He took a deep breath and sighed. 'I'm happy to sit with Blossom. I need to decide the best time to reinsert her feeding tube. I'll let Ron know that if her mum wants to talk to the doctor on duty, I'm happy to go down after he has.'

She could tell that it pained him to say that. Dougie was probably normally the guy who liked to be in charge of everything. But he had to think what was best for the patient.

She watched as he went over and had a discussion with Ron. She could tell instantly that Ron was happy with the decision. He took another instant picture of Blossom, and once Dougie had settled next to the incubator hurried out of the door.

Silence fell over the unit once more. The only noises were the quiet hisses and beeps of pumps, monitors and ventilators.

Alice could sense that Dougie's eyes were

on her. But she didn't turn. She didn't look at him. He'd annoyed her tonight, and she wanted him to know it.

So she held her head high and walked back over to the babies in her care and did her job.

CHAPTER FIVE

A WEEK HAD passed and there was still an awkward silence in the townhouse. Alice and Dougie worked around each other with barely a murmur. Alice was still mad, Dougie resolute, both understanding each other a little but determined in their stance.

Dougie was sitting at the table in the kitchen, eating some eggs for breakfast and searching the internet for places to visit in Washington. He had the next couple of days off and wanted to get a better feel for the city. The Lincoln Memorial and Smithsonian were on his radar, but his interest had been piqued by the few different places that Alice had mentioned previously.

She moved silently into the kitchen and picked up the percolator, pouring some coffee into a cup and adding some sweetener. As she toasted some bread, her phone sounded. She'd left it sitting at the edge of the table and Dougie's head lifted automatically. There was a picture on the screen but he couldn't see what it was. Alice continued what she was doing, then turned around and glanced at her phone. He couldn't pretend not to notice how her expression changed. She swiped her screen and shoved the phone into the back pocket of her denim shorts.

'Okay?' He couldn't help himself.

For a few moments all he could see was her back as she put her toast on a plate, then turned and brought it to the table with some butter and jam from the fridge.

It was almost as if something had washed over her, but in a resigned kind of way. 'Just someone thinking they're funny,' was all she said.

As she started eating her toast she looked up at him. 'Where are you going today?' She must have realised he was off.

'Haven't decided yet,' he said. He swung his tablet around. 'Was contemplating a few of these places.'

She looked over and pointed. 'No, not as good as it sounds; this one is interesting—and that one is definitely worth the trip.' After a few seconds she gave a sigh. 'I promised I'd show you around.'

He felt her soften at the edges a little. Dou-

gie didn't mind exploring Washington himself, but having a guide would be much more
interesting. 'You did,' he agreed.

She kept eating, clearly thinking carefully.
Dougie kept silent.

'I think if we can spend the day not talking about work, this could be fine,' she said.
It was as if she were drawing an invisible
line in the sand.

'Happy not to talk about work,' he said,
lifting his cup and plate and loading them
into the dishwasher, before turning around
and folding his arms.

He was struck by how attractive she was.
Her hair was swept up in a ponytail high on
her head but, instead of the regular way she
wore it at work, this was much bigger and
bouffant. It reminded him of a picture he'd
seen years ago of Jackie O. She was wearing
a bright orange top that sat just off her shoulders, long gold earrings, her denim shorts
that revealed tanned slim legs and a pair of
trainers. Deep down, something curled in
his stomach, recognising that he was finding Alice attractive.

Alarm bells sounded in his head. There
was a reason he didn't date colleagues. He'd
learned his lesson the hard way. He couldn't
let some casual attraction to a colleague lead

to anything that could ruin his six-month placement, and his reputation at Wald. He gave a silent sigh as he tried to rid himself of the weight on his shoulders. All of those things mattered. But he could be friends with his housemate. He could go sightseeing across the city. There was nothing in that— was there?

He made up his mind. 'Where are we going to go?'

She swung her legs out from underneath the table with a smile. 'Oh, you can just wait and see. Let me grab my bag.'

Dougie finished clearing the kitchen and grabbed his wallet. Alice appeared next to him with a small bag at her hip, the long strap across her body, and a pair of sunglasses perched on her head. 'Ready?'

He nodded and locked the door behind them as they headed out onto the street.

He was happy to let her take the lead and, after some subway rides and some walking, she smiled as she waved her hand at a sign for the National Museum of Health and Medicine.

'Isn't this work-related?' he asked as they made their way inside.

'But not specific to our work. Your eyes

will boggle at some of the stuff they have in here.'

She wasn't joking. It was like walking through the history of medicine, and Dougie couldn't even try to pretend that he didn't love it. Some of the exhibits were ancient, some from the World Wars. The exhibits of the effects of atomic weapons were heart-wrenching, the research on tuberculosis and the initial discoveries that mosquitoes carried disease were fascinating. Then came the fragments of bullet that had killed Abraham Lincoln, along with pieces of skull. Then there was the malformed megacolon removed from a man with constipation and, last but not least, the completely and utterly hideous stomach-sized hairball from a teenage girl who'd eaten her hair for six years, that left an eye-watering impression.

By the time they got back outside, Dougie was glad to be in fresh air again. 'It's like the exhibits in the Surgeons' Hall Museums back in Edinburgh,' he said to Alice. 'Whilst some of them are fascinating, you've got to question how some of them got here. And how people thought at that time.'

'Makes me glad we've got the technology we have,' she replied. 'So much of this would be discovered early and be able to be treated.

The history of medicine and human development is not kind.'

He gave her a sideways glance and a smile. 'Absolutely. Kind of overwhelming. Where to next?'

She gave a thoughtful nod. 'Okay, how about we take a true breather and go somewhere with a spectacular view for lunch, then we could go to the Botanic Gardens? It means a bit of travel. Are you up for it?'

'Sure.' He shrugged. 'Why not?'

They spent the next hour on the subway and got into a good-natured fight about the best ever sci-fi film made, closely followed by the best ever sci-fi series. It was a closely fought battle between *Star Wars* and *The Search for Spock* and *Close Encounters*. Some other people on the subway joined in, all debating the best ever starship captain, with a twelve-year-old girl with thick glasses giving an impassioned debate for Captain Janeway. Dougie and Alice were still laughing as they emerged from the subway.

'Always Picard,' said Dougie. 'But I didn't want to break her heart.'

His phone sounded and in the blink of an eye Alice groaned. '*Beverly Hills Cop*? You really need to up your game.'

'I'll do my best.' He smiled, pleased that

they seemed back on much better terms now. The sun was shining high in the sky, and she'd brought them back out into the middle of the city. 'Where to now?'

She pointed upwards. 'We're going up there. The cafeteria on the sixth floor has floor-to-ceiling windows with spectacular views of the city.'

'Sold,' he said instantly, looking at another sign. 'Thought you were taking me to Library of Congress to see the Gutenberg Bible.'

She waved her hand. 'That's for another day. One where you can give it your full attention. Today's priority is food.'

They took the elevator to the sixth floor and walked out into the wide space of the cafeteria. The food was simple but wide-ranging enough for anyone to find something to their liking. With a hot chicken sandwich for Alice and a Philly cheesesteak sandwich for him, and some diet sodas, they sat down at one of the windows overlooking the city.

'I like it up here,' said Alice. 'Sometimes it can be overrun with school trips. But the food is reasonable, and I've brought a book up here before.'

He looked at her with interest. 'You brought a book to the library?'

'Absolutely,' she said. 'What better place

to read? And I'm not the only one who likes to do it. Look around. Some of these people are staffers from Capitol Hill. There aren't too many places to eat around here. But the rest—the ones who clearly aren't visitors? They're like me. Just here for the view and the food.'

He looked around and she was right. There were a number of people—mainly on their own, sipping coffee or eating a muffin, reading a book.

'Are you really an old soul at heart?'

She wrinkled her brow for a second, then smiled. 'I think I probably am. Penny would probably laugh at that, though. I like a bit of time, a bit of space. But she doesn't always acknowledge that; she still calls me dating central.'

At those words, Dougie gave a swallow and mentioned the subject that had been bothering him. 'Is everything okay with that? I've noted you deleting a few apps.'

She sighed and pressed her lips together. He knew she was trying to figure out what to tell him.

He didn't want to press. And whether Alice did or didn't date was none of his business—something he knew entirely, but strangely annoyed him. He held up one hand. 'Just tell me if there's anything you need to tell me. I'm not being nosey. We're trying to be friends.' Then he said something that worried him most. 'If ever you don't feel safe, you let me know.'

She reached for her soda and there was a slight tremor to her hand. 'Okay.' The word came out much sooner than he'd expected, and with a hint of shakiness.

So now he wanted to know everything. Should he say something to Penny? But no. They were sisters. And they clearly had a bond. Alice spoke to her sister a couple of times a day. Penny would likely know everything about this, and just tell Dougie it was none of his business.

But why did the fact that Alice had fixed her gaze out of the windows and across the city bother him? This whole subject had made her edgy. It shouldn't. She should feel free to date whoever and whenever she pleased.

It suddenly struck him that, even though he'd been here a few weeks now, she'd never mentioned going out on a date. 'You got yoga tonight?' he asked, remembering she sometimes went to a class with a friend.

Alice shook her head. 'Not tonight. Carol has something on with her family. In fact, I was thinking if I haven't killed you by the end of the day, there might be a good place we could go to round off the evening.'

'Do I need to check if you're planning on killing me by exhausting me with our touring around Washington, or if this is just killing me in general?'

She smiled and gathered their plates from lunch. 'Not sure yet. Guess we'll just wait and see how it goes.' There was something teasing in her tone, and the smile she was giving him sent a wave of tingles across his skin. As he stood, she moved alongside him, her arm brushing against his as she pointed at something just a little away from them. 'That's where we're headed next. The Botanic Gardens is only a short walk away.'

As they wandered back outside, the air was still warm. Dougie gave a laugh and made a show of fanning himself. 'Spring in Scotland is usually wind and rain with an occasional bout of sunshine.'

'Well, spring in Washington can equal sweltering days and cooler evenings. This heat isn't unusual at all.'

They walked along the street towards the Botanic Gardens. Alice seemed more relaxed. She hadn't looked at her phone once since they'd left the house. Maybe she'd put it on silent. But whatever had been bothering her before seemed to have been forgotten about now. Dougie was glad. The more time he spent around Alice, the more protective of her he found himself. She was a beautiful woman, with an edge of stubbornness that he actually liked. She could give him a run for his money with an eighties movie marathon, and would probably beat him at any eighties music quiz. He liked the way she was happy to argue with him and stand her ground. It didn't make him shift his position, but that didn't matter. She had an easy way with patients, and clearly adored the babies she cared for. She was intelligent, and gorgeous. Sharing a place with her meant his thoughts occasionally strayed where they shouldn't. But no one knew that but him. There were times when her brown eyes held his gaze for a fraction longer than necessary, or her words had a teasing edge to them. For the first time in a long time it made him wonder about a workmate. He'd never dated anyone from work since Kayla. He had dated other women. Sienna, who worked in cyber security, and then Julie, who was a professional tennis coach in London. But neither relationship had given the same kind of sparks he felt around Alice. He was doing his best to ignore everything about this. But walking with her in the sunshine, playing tourist in her city and being in her company this long—made her hard to ignore.

They entered the beautiful gardens, with paths throughout and a large conservatory in the distance.

'It's nice just to walk, isn't it?' said Alice. Dougie was so easy to be around.

He bent over to take a closer look at one of the flowers. 'Wondered what that one was called,' he murmured.

'You like flowers and plants?'

He waggled one hand from side to side. 'I don't have a garden in London, but the house my mum and dad have in Scotland has an enormous garden. I played in it when I was young. We had brambles, raspberry bushes, apple and pear trees and a whole row of cherry blossom trees.' He glanced around. 'The cherry blossoms around Washington remind me of home.'

Alice stopped for a minute and inhaled deeply, letting the scents wash over her. They were next to a bed of red tulips, each one immaculate. 'We moved around a lot as kids. Most Army houses did have gardens, but we weren't really there long enough to plant and grow plants or trees.' She envied the fact he'd had a large play area at his fingertips.

'What were your favourite flowers?'

He blinked for a minute and she realised it was an unusual question for a man. But Dougie seemed as at ease as ever. 'That's simple. I like colour. Livingstone daisies.'

She wrinkled her nose and he pulled out his phone and typed something in. 'They might have a different name.' He turned the phone around to reveal the pinks, yellows, whites and oranges of the small flowers. 'Yip, one I can't pronounce.'

She touched his screen. 'They're beautiful. I've heard the name, but couldn't remember what they look like.'

She pulled up her own phone. 'That's weird. The one I like best looks like a daisy too. Here—' She swung her phone around to show him the orange gerberas. 'I only have pots at the entrance to the townhouse and have tried a few times to grow them, but my doorstep is directly in the sun and they always seem to die after a few weeks, which is why I've only got lavender right now. I guess I'm just not as green-fingered as I'd like to be.'

They'd walked near to the entrance of the conservatory. She grinned at him. 'Wait until we get inside. But be warned, at one point you might need to hold your nose.'

Dougie frowned. 'What?'

She laughed. 'It's a surprise; come on.'

Alice had been through this conservatory a dozen times already this year, so she knew exactly where she was going. They moved past orchids and ferns before Dougie gave a cough. His nose wrinkled.

'What is that?'

Other people had scarves or masks around their faces. The closer they got, the stronger the smell.

They rounded another corner and Alice pointed to the giant, oddly shaped flower. 'Meet *amorphophallus titanum*,' she said.

Dougie coughed again as he tilted his head to look at the flower. 'Did you just say phallus?'

She laughed. 'I did.'

His eyes darted between her and the giant flower. 'It does look a bit like…' He let his words trail off. 'But the smell…' His hand was up at his nose.

She smiled. 'Yip, when it blooms it smells like rotting flesh. We call it the corpse flower.'

Even though the smell was horrific, there were still a number of curious tourists taking pictures of the burgundy bloom. Alice reached out and grabbed Dougie's hand, pulling him towards the nearest exit. When they got outside she dropped his hand, but was aware of the empty feeling in her palm.

'This is where you bring me?' he asked. 'I get you to show me the secrets around Washington, and you bring me to a flower that looks like a penis and smells like a rotting corpse.'

As they burst out into the fresh air, Alice doubled over laughing. 'You're a medic. I knew you could take it. Plus, don't let it be said that I don't take you to the best places.'

They were back outside now, surrounded by lush lawns and flower beds filled with rainbows of colour. 'Now this—' Dougie held out his hands '—is beautiful. This is a pleasant walk. A place to get to know someone. Take a seat, while away the day. *That*—' he turned around and pointed '—is a scene from a horror movie. I'm just waiting for the axe-murderer to jump out and chase us.'

He was play-acting, and she knew it. What was more, she liked it. She'd liked being around this guy all day. The work stuff had been pushed to one side, even though she knew it would likely crop up again. For now, she was forgetting about the fact they worked together, forgetting about the complicating factor that they were sharing a place. Right now, she was just concentrating on the chemistry in the air between them.

'Had enough yet?' she teased. 'Or are you brave enough to continue?'

He leaned forward, closer than she expected. 'You have more?'

Part of his dark hair fell across his brow. She resisted the itch in her fingers to reach out and push it back. She focused on his lips. 'I have a lot more.' She couldn't help the way the words came out. She hadn't meant them to sound sexy, but the implication was there before she even really knew it.

Dougie froze. The sides of his mouth lifted slowly. He didn't pull back, just kept looking at her with those flashing blue eyes. Whether she'd meant the implication or not was irrelevant because it was there, and it seemed as if he'd reached out and grabbed it.

Alice was holding her breath. She was thanking her lucky stars that he hadn't jumped back and laughed it off like some stupid joke. That would have made her feel about two feet tall.

She hadn't misread anything. The looks. The brushed arms and hands.

He kept still. 'Okay then.' His voice was low and husky. He reached out and took her hand. A very deliberate act. She'd grabbed him first. But that had been just to get him through the crowds and to the way out of the conservatory. This was much more.

'Where to?' he asked.

Alice breathed out slowly, her brain misting for a few seconds. Then she instantly remembered her original plan. 'Okay.' She smiled as they started walking. 'We're heading back to Foggy Bottom. I'm going to show the hidden gem we try not to tell others about.'

'Lead the way.'

The subway was busy, and they ended up crushed next to each other. But neither objected. The air between them had changed. Her head was confused. She didn't want to get close to any man. The dating apps allowed her to keep all men at a real distance. After last time, she was scared to let her guard down—scared to trust whether she should allow any man to get close to her. So why on earth was she letting Dougie hold her hand?

She hated being confused like this. She felt safe around Dougie. But what if she'd got that wrong? What if her instincts about him were wrong?

She swallowed and looked down at their joined hands. Dougie was looking in the other direction, talking freely to another Scot he'd just met on the subway. She took a deep breath, telling herself this was nothing. This was only a first step. She could pull back any time she wanted. Those thoughts washed over her, stopping the rise of panic and giving her the reassurance that she needed.

Alice looked down at her clothes as they left the subway and made a quick call on her phone. It was the first time she'd looked at it all day. She was thankful there was nothing on the screen. 'Maris, it's me. Can I come along in twenty minutes?'

When she heard the news she wanted, she turned back to Dougie. 'Okay, so we're going somewhere a little more upscale. There isn't officially a dress code, but I guess shorts might be pushing it.' She started hurrying along the street towards the townhouse.

Dougie looked curious. 'I need trousers?'

She nodded. 'Yes, pants.'

He shuddered. 'That word means something a whole lot different in Scotland. Trousers. I need trousers.'

'Keep telling yourself that.' She laughed as she opened the front door to the townhouse. 'Now, you need to be ready in ten minutes.'

'I'll beat you,' he said casually as his long legs started to stride up the stairs.

'No way,' she joked as she ran up behind him and ducked into her room.

Less than ten minutes later they were back by the front door. Dougie had changed into black trousers and a black shirt open at the neck. Alice had grabbed the first dress in her closet. It hadn't been out in some time. But the red slash-neck dress with a dipping back had always been easy to wear. She'd slid her feet into black strappy sandals, not too high for the quick walk ahead, and brushed some powder on her face, along with some red lipstick. Her hair had to stick to the same style from earlier today. There was no time for a refresh.

'Are you going to tell me where we're going?'

She shook her head. 'But it's fun. You'll like it. I have a friend who works there.'

'That's who you called earlier?'

She nodded as they walked down the street. 'You have to reserve in advance, but Maris always finds room for me.' She held out her hand. 'Maybe we should have brought jackets. It can get really cool in the evenings.'

'It's not too bad,' started Dougie, then stopped and looked at her. 'Ah, so we'll be outside?'

'Maybe.' They kept walking and she led him into a luxurious hotel.

Dougie gave a low wolf whistle. 'This place is nice.'

The elevator took them to the roof and Alice walked ahead and out to the roof-top bar. 'Now, this is the best kept secret in Foggy Bottom.' She smiled as she held out her arms and spun around to face him.

Dougie's eyes were wide. The bar, based on a balcony, overlooked the Potomac River. There was a collection of low couches and some high tables and chairs. The area was edged by a smoked glass safety barrier that zigzagged around the roof, set with white lights.

'Definitely nice,' he murmured. 'I imagine it looks just as good from the river as it does from here.' His arm slid around Alice's waist.

A woman with blonde hair and a smart black uniform gave Alice a wave and walked over, kissing her on both cheeks. She held out her hand to Dougie. 'Maris Cairns. I know all of Alice's secrets and I can be bought with candy.'

Alice's stomach fluttered. She could tell from the expression on Maris's face that she approved already.

Dougie laughed. 'You're clearly secret

twins, since I already know that Alice can be bought with candy too.'

Maris's eyes widened and she gave Alice a gentle slap on the arm. 'Oh, you didn't warn me about the accent. You've got your own Sean Connery.'

Alice met his gaze. *The Untouchables,'* she said. 'There's an eighties movie we haven't watched yet. We can watch that one later tonight.'

Maris looked at them both with amusement. 'Cosy,' she remarked, before leading them over to a high table next to the glass surround. She handed them drink menus. 'What would you like?'

Alice pondered for a moment. 'It's either white wine or the cocktail of the day.'

Maris smiled. 'It's Sunset Blaze—spiced rum, grenadine, orange juice, club soda and lime.'

'Sold,' said Alice immediately.

'And what about you?' Maris asked Dougie.

'I'll just have a beer, thanks.'

Maris disappeared and they settled on the stools looking over the river. The sun was dipping in the sky, sending purple and orange streaks across the water. 'This is a spectacular view,' said Dougie.

Alice nodded in appreciation. 'This is one of the few places that the locals like to come. Most of the high-end hotels around here only cater for their guests. But this place realised early on it could capture a bit of what was missing for the local residents. Somewhere trendy, not completely out of the price zone and somewhere spectacular to sit.'

'Do you come here a lot?' Dougie asked.

Her skin prickled. Was he asking if she'd brought other dates here? Because that was what this was—wasn't it? A date?

'If I'm meeting girlfriends, we frequently come here. It's a nice environment.' She pointed to a room through some glass doors. 'There's a whisky lounge through there if the weather is being difficult. But mainly we just like to sit out here, drink wine and cocktails and watch the world on the river.' She licked her lips as she looked around. 'It feels safe here. Obviously Maris is behind the bar tonight, but even when she's not, the staff here are good with locals. They shut down anyone who's getting a bit...forward,' she finished.

Alice was feeling totally relaxed in Dougie's company, so when she was met with silence she realised what she'd just said. Maris appeared and set down their drinks and some nuts before moving away.

Alice took a sip of her cocktail. 'Delicious,' she said. When she looked up, she could see his gaze fixed on her, worry creasing his forehead.

'Safe,' he repeated slowly. 'Are there places around here you don't feel safe?'

'Well, no, but I mean there's always places in every city that aren't too safe…' She was babbling now and she knew it. 'But this place is good like that. I've never felt as if I had anything to worry about when I'm here.'

Darn it. She hadn't really wanted to talk about the fact she'd literally found herself casing every joint she'd walked into since the stalking incident. Looking for anyone out of place, or anyone who could cause trouble. Several times in the last year, she'd encouraged friends to move on from places where there were large groups of rowdy men, or others on their own that stared for too long. All things she would never have considered in the past. She hated that one incident with someone had made her wary of the world.

Dougie's words were measured. 'I get that safety is an issue for everyone these days. And I'm glad you've found a place that you feel safe in. Everyone should have a place like that.' He looked around appreciatively. 'And this is certainly a beautiful place.'

They both watched as some boats and a group of canoes came along the darkening river. Quiet music played in the background, mixing with the conversation around them and the sounds from the river beneath. 'I get why you like this place.'

'See—' smiled Alice '—I saved the best for last.'

'I thought you claimed the corpse flower was the best?'

'I was just keeping you on your toes. There's still plenty more to see around Washington.'

'I think I'm going to stick to the more traditional venues next time. I've still to go to the Lincoln Memorial and the Smithsonian.'

'You'll like them too. I just wanted you to see the quaint and cute. The things you probably wouldn't see on your own.'

As he looked at her, she could sense something change between them again. He reached over and touched her hand. 'I really appreciate what you did today. I've had fun.'

'So have I.' The words came out a little hoarser than she meant them to. But her vocal cords had decided to panic at the way he was looking at her.

It wasn't as if it hadn't happened before. Of course a guy had looked at her before, in a way that meant she knew entirely what might happen next.

She kept her hand exactly where it was. His hand was resting over hers lightly, his thumb tracing circles around the edge of one finger.

'Can we do it again?' he asked.

Every part of her wanted to scream *Yes*— even though she didn't usually get involved with anyone at work. But it had worked for her sister. Penny had met the love of her life at work. Now she and Benedict were happily engaged. And Alice wasn't even considering any of that. All she was contemplating here was a kiss. And kissing Dougie MacLachlan was certainly appealing.

Her throat was dry, her barriers still in place. Moving them even a little lower would be a huge step. Could she trust Dougie? Could she trust his intentions? Could she trust herself?

He'd always made her feel safe. Even though they battled at work, she'd never felt worried around him. It made her realise that she might have more trouble trusting herself than him. She said the words out loud, even though she still had reservations.

'I think that might work,' she said, unable to keep the smile out of her voice.

The connection between them was electric. Both stood at the same time and Dougie pulled her towards him. His hand slipped to her lower back as their mouths connected.

She could taste the cold beer on his lips. Her hands moved, first resting on his shoulders and then sliding around his neck.

She was conscious of where they were— somewhere very public. And the thoughts she was having right now weren't public in the slightest.

She pulled back from him, taking a breath and resting her head against his. 'Whoa,' she said softly.

Dougie didn't say a word, just gave her a slow smile and pulled out his wallet to cover the bill. Then he slid his hand into hers and led her out of the bar.

CHAPTER SIX

Dougie was settling into the way of things in the NICU in Washington. He'd had time to look at all the protocols and procedures within the unit and had been happy to see that they were regularly updated and reviewed by a multi-disciplinary team.

He'd made a few suggestions to Tara, the charge nurse, about the layout of some of the paper recording sheets kept at the foot of each incubator. She'd listened and taken on board his suggestions, reviewing them alongside the staff and producing some new templates to trial for a month. It had been entirely minor, but he'd noticed a few staff forgot to record some details on the other side of one of the charts. Reviewing the layout and bringing it all onto one page would hopefully stop that happening.

So whilst his work life was going well, his personal life was going even better. But there was no doubt in Dougie's mind that he still had trust issues. Alice was feisty and occasionally lazy. She was meticulous at work at all times. But on her time off she could spend days where she was up early in the morning and keep going until last thing at night, but she also had days where she could drink diet soda, snack on some chocolate and have a giant book or movie binge.

Their first kiss had resulted in a strained farewell on the stairs that night. Since then, they'd become more comfortable around each other in the house. Dougie was careful not to push and let things go at a pace they were both comfortable with. Last night they'd started watching a movie, but then spent most of the night kissing on the sofa. It was amazing how many hours could be spent just concentrating on the perfect kiss—and at this stage he was sure they had aced it.

But it didn't stop the worries circulating in his head. He had doubts. And he hated himself for that. It was as if there was a silent voice always whispering *Are you sure?* in his head. He didn't think Alice was anything like Kayla. But the idea of trusting someone after everything that had happened with her was hard. Really hard.

Today, they were both working again. Both

were careful around each other in the work-place. Everyone knew they were living to-gether, but neither felt ready to share that things might be moving on between them and, to be honest, that suited him.

The conversation around this had been easy for them both. 'I don't want anyone at work to know about us,' Alice had said. 'I don't want anyone's opinion or comments.'

'Me neither,' he'd agreed. 'Let's just keep what's happening between us just between us. At least until we know what this is.'

They'd agreed with a kiss. A very long kiss, and that had been fine.

Truth was, Dougie didn't know how things might develop between them. A one-night stand wasn't on the agenda. Something for a few weeks might be fun, or even something for the duration of Dougie's contract, which was six months. But he hadn't even consid-ered what he might do next. His contract had an option to extend, but he wasn't sure if his long-term future would be in the US, as op-posed to London, Scotland or anywhere else. And it was clear to him that, after years of being an Army kid, Alice had put down firm roots in Washington. Neither of them was ready for that kind of conversation yet.

He also wondered if his brain would ever

stop questioning itself again. The barriers he'd put in place since the incident with Kayla were deeper rooted than he'd ever realised. He'd imagined if he met someone again he'd eventually be able to throw off his trust issues and doubts. But he was struggling to adjust. Maybe it was because he worked with Alice and the added complications would always be there. No matter how comfortable he tried to be in this relationship.

The morning had been relatively calm in the NICU so far. Dougie was just reviewing some charts when the phone rang.

'NICU. Dr MacLachlan.'

'This is Rhonda from the ER. We have a pregnant woman on the way in following an RTA. Paramedics are reporting severe trauma, with the potential for immediate delivery. ETA ten minutes. Can we have a neonatologist and NICU nurse for emergency theatre?'

'Absolutely, be there in a few minutes.'

He replaced the receiver and relayed the message to Tara. She took one look around the unit. 'Take Alice with you and I'll get someone to cover your patients. Let me know how it goes. We have a spot available if required.'

He nodded and hurried over to Alice, touching her elbow and telling her the news.

They ran down the corridor and stairs towards the emergency theatre, meeting one of the obstetricians, who was talking into a phone, giving instructions.

Both Dougie and Alice were already wearing scrubs, but dived into the nearest locker room to grab a clean set and pull on surgical hats. They were at sinks scrubbing a few moments later as one of the other staff wheeled an incubator in.

The obstetrician had started scrubbing with the phone tucked between her ear and neck. One of the other staff was tucking her hair under a hat.

'Any more information?' Dougie asked.

The obstetrician finally stopped speaking and turned to face them, her face pale, worry lines deep in her brow. 'Sorry, I'm Val Kearney. Mom is being resuscitated after being cut out the car. It will need to be an immediate Caesarean section. I can't even tell you her gestation right now.'

She took a deep breath and looked around at the staff. 'Everyone please prepare—we have around two minutes. Ambulance is pulling into the ER bay now.'

There was silence. Even though her face was hidden behind a mask, he could see the worry on Alice's face. Staff from NICU could be called at short notice to an emergency delivery. But he didn't know how often she'd been in Theatre and how she would cope with a situation like this.

His own stomach was clenching uncomfortably. No one wanted to hear the news that a pregnant woman was being resuscitated. A door opened and a man, fully gowned and masked, walked through. 'Leo Atwell,' he said. 'General surgeon. I've been asked to assist.' He nodded to the obstetrician. 'Obviously, you go first. But tell me if I can do anything to assist. As soon as baby is out, I'll see if I can do anything to save mom.'

One of the nurses gave a shout. 'We have a positive ID on mom. Lila Higgins, age thirty-four. Hospital records show this is her second pregnancy, nothing untoward noted, expecting a boy and she's thirty-three weeks. She's normally under Dr Amjad.'

There was a nodding of heads. Val moved over to the theatre table. 'Someone let Dr Amjad know the situation with his patient, please.'

For the next few seconds there was silence, with all eyes on the door.

Dougie took a few deep breaths. Calm was what was needed. These people were professionals. They could do this.

The doors burst open. A paramedic was on top doing chest compressions. A doctor was alongside; it was clear he'd got IV access. Another nurse was at the top of the trolley, bagging the patient.

Everyone jumped down and there was a simultaneous movement to slide Lila Higgins onto the theatre trolley. With low voices, everyone did their role. The anaesthetist took over the airway. Theatre nurses cut clothes and attached monitor leads. Dougie and Alice stood back, ready for the next step, waiting to receive the baby.

Lila's stomach was wiped with antiseptic solution as the resus continued. Val Kearney waited for a nod from the anaesthetist and, in what felt like moments, had the little boy out. She placed him into Dougie's waiting hands.

From that point on, all Dougie's and Alice's focus was on the little boy. He was floppy and blue to begin with, but quickly began to pick up. Breathing started with little assistance, oxygen support was given and Alice attached the monitors and read out all of the recordings. A third member of staff charted everything as they talked out loud. Dougie was impressed by how methodical Alice was. She was completely focused and a perfect assistant. As they worked together to establish the condition of the baby, it was as if she read his mind.

They could hear quiet chaos going on behind them, but neither turned around. Once they were happy that their patient was stabilised enough to transfer up to the NICU, Dougie finally looked over his shoulder.

Leo Atwell was working carefully, as units of blood were going in on both sides, and Val was stitching up the uterus. 'Clamp,' he said quietly.

'There's a lot of blood,' whispered Alice.

Dougie nodded. 'It must be her spleen or liver that was damaged in the accident. I hope he can manage to get the bleeding under control.'

Alice fastened the identity band around the tiny wrist. The resuscitation was continuing and tension was mounting. Dougie put his hand on Alice's shoulder. Neither of them had any idea how long the resuscitation had been going before Lila was brought into the theatre.

'Halt,' came the firm voice of Leo Atwell. There was silence for a second, then a slow beep-beep was heard from one of the monitors.

Lila had a heartbeat again. When Dougie looked back over, Val had finished stitching and was round next to Leo, holding a clamp. Dougie couldn't imagine that these two surgeons had ever worked together before, but both were doing their absolute best to give this mum a fighting chance.

As the heartbeat continued, both lifted their heads. 'How's our boy?' asked Val. It was clear that up until this point they'd been just as focused as Dougie and Alice had. Patients always came first.

'Stable enough to transfer up to NICU,' said Dougie.

'Wonderful.' Val nodded. 'Go on up, and we'll let you know how things go with mom.'

Alice moved to a nearby phone on the wall and let Tara know they were coming up. The theatre had a set of elevators exclusively for use for patients and they moved the incubator into one of those. As the doors closed, both pulled off their masks.

Alice moved over and hugged Dougie. It was clear that relief was flooding through both of them. 'Welcome to the world, little guy,' said Dougie, looking down at the baby boy. 'We're hoping your mum or dad will get a chance to give you a name soon.'

Alice wiped her eyes. 'That was horrendous. I feel as if I've gone ten rounds in a boxing ring.' She pulled her watch from her pocket and shook her head. 'It's barely been an hour since we got the initial call.'

Dougie shook his head. 'This little guy was so lucky. He perked up so quickly, and at thirty-three weeks here's hoping we won't have too many complications.'

The hug felt good. It was only for a few moments, but it felt good to have someone to hold onto right now. Lots of staff found it hard to explain the huge adrenaline rushes of reacting to emergencies, followed by the lows that came after. The only people who really understood were those who worked alongside. He put a kiss on her nose, then released Alice before the elevator doors slid back open. Both of them moved instantly back to their positions at the side of the incubator and wheeled it quickly down the corridor to NICU, where their colleagues were waiting.

Tara and a fellow doctor took a handover report and then she gave them both a nod. 'Go and take a break. I know how these things are. I'll see if I can find out any more from the theatre staff.'

Dougie looked reluctantly at the little boy they'd just seen delivered. He wanted to stay. He wanted to make sure everything was done exactly the way he thought it should be, but he knew he had to trust his fellow colleagues.

And Tara was right. She wanted to give them both some time to decompress. It was likely that at some point the whole team—ER, theatre, obstetrics and NICU staff—would be asked to get together and learn from today.

Alice came over and gave him a nudge. 'I want some coffee, and some dessert. Let's take five.'

Dougie nodded and grabbed his jacket, ensuring he had his wallet. She looked at him in surprise. 'Let's go a bit further than the canteen.'

She gave a nod. 'Let me get my jacket.' She turned towards Tara to tell her they might be a bit longer, but it seemed that Tara had already guessed as she gave a wave of her hand, telling them to go on.

Dougie walked down the corridor with Alice and as they stepped into the elevator he slipped his hand into hers. She looked up at him in surprise, but didn't pull her hand away. She just moved closer, her shoulder pressing against his. It was a big hospital. Someone might see them together, but equally they might be anonymous to all those around them.

When they reached the ground floor, Dougie walked in long strides across the main foyer and led her out, turning left, then crossing the street to a bakery.

She reached her other hand over and grasped his arm, smiling in delight as they walked through the door and were greeted with the smells of warm bread, sweet cakes and good coffee.

It was a place most of the hospital staff loved but rarely had time to visit during the day. The woman behind the counter gave them a wide smile, clocked their uniforms and nodded to a table. There were other people in the bakery, but the woman came over immediately, as if she realised time would be a priority. 'What can I get you both?'

Alice's eyes looked over at the glass-fronted cabinet. Dougie knew that she'd been in here before and would likely have a favourite dessert. 'Can I have a skinny latte with an extra shot, and a slice of the pecan pie, please?'

'With cream?'

'Oh, go on then,' Alice said, smiling.

'I'll have a cappuccino, and a piece of the apple and caramel pie.' He gave a nod before she asked. 'And yes, with cream, please.'

The bakery owner smiled. 'Be right with you.'

As she walked away Alice reached over

and threaded her fingers through Dougie's. 'I'm praying,' she murmured in a low voice. 'Praying for that poor mom, her new baby, her other kid and the poor father, who will be having a heart attack when he hears what's happened to his family.'

Dougie swallowed, his mouth dry. He squeezed her fingers. 'I get that. I've seen a lot of things in my time. But that has to be the most traumatic delivery ever.' He spoke carefully. 'But our little guy? He could be fine. Time will tell. He was flat to begin with, and we don't know if there was a lack of oxygen to him while his mum was being treated. But his recovery was good and he stabilised really quickly. Everything up until that point in the pregnancy seems to have been fine.'

Alice blinked. There were tears pooling in her eyes. 'I hate that bit,' she admitted. 'The part where someone does everything possible to do things right and live a healthy life, then something happens completely out of their control. And that's it. It can mean life or death.'

She looked up as the waitress came back with the coffees and pie. She shook her head as she picked up her fork. 'It's kind of ironic, isn't it, that I'm talking about a healthy life-style when I'm about to eat pie.'

'We've had a big morning. We need something to give us a boost. And you are healthy. You're the one with your yoga mat out every other morning, twisting into positions that make my eyes water. You're the one that does those strange noodly vegetable things when you should be using spaghetti.'

She laughed. 'Carrot and courgette is good for you.'

'Not when it's paired with bolognaise.'

She smiled, but they stared at each other for a few moments, then ate some of their pie, still holding hands.

This was something entirely new to Dougie. He'd spent time with colleagues before after a traumatic event. He'd held a crying medical student who'd had to deal with the death of someone her own age. He'd sat next to an older doctor who'd had to debrief a whole team after one of their members of staff had been attacked and seriously injured.

But he hadn't done *this*. He hadn't watched a young mum being resuscitated while her baby was delivered. He hadn't sat later with someone he cared about. Someone he'd thought about during the events and hoped they would be okay.

Alice sipped her coffee and gave him a smile. 'I want you to know that you have permission to make the next few days nice and quiet.'

'I do?'

'Yip. Once we get back upstairs and sort out our boy, I'm going to spend the rest of the day with the twins. Angie's starting to open up a little now. I'm pretty sure she's been bulimic in the past. She's feeling a lot of guilt about the twins right now, and I'm trying to encourage her to speak to one of the counsellors.'

'She's such a sad girl. So lonely. I hate that she has so little support.'

'I'm trying to strike a balance with her. Angie needs to recognise what she needs and be willing to have it. I don't want to force anything onto her. She's vulnerable enough. I think if I try and push her to attend groups or accept help from different agencies she might withdraw further. I want Angie to feel confident in herself. Confident that she can look after these babies and give them what they need. Of course, I think she needs some assistance, but I want her to feel comfortable enough that when we offer it she doesn't think it's a reflection on her. That will take time.'

'She's lucky to have such a good nurse.' Dougie smiled. He loved the passion that came into Alice's eyes when she talked about one of her patients and her commitment to doing the best job she could.

Alice gave a half-hearted smile. 'I don't get it.'

'Get what?' he asked.

'I know some of our colleagues get a buzz out of emergency situations. The adrenaline, the rush.' She shook her head. 'But just not me. I was terrified in the theatre. And when our little guy came out all limp...' Her voice tailed off.

He gave a slow nod. 'I know. I get it. It was completely and utterly terrifying.'

She lifted her head in surprise. 'You too?'

He smiled at her. 'One hundred per cent. I've looked after a lot of babies born in emergency situations. I've been called to Theatre a lot. But generally it's because the mum or baby have become suddenly unwell during the labour process. I've never had someone brought in who was being resuscitated. I only hope she can't remember a single thing about it—' he squeezed Alice's hand again '—and she wakes up and realises that she has a beautiful son, who is doing fine.'

He knew it was all wishful thinking, but

the wonders of modern medicine meant he could actually say those words. There was a chance that both of those things could turn out to be true—her surviving and her baby being fine.

He looked down at their coffee cups and plates. 'We should go back.'

Alice nodded. 'Yeah, we should. I'm kind of scared to find out what happens next.'

Dougie gave a nod as he stood up and left some money for the bill. He paused for a second, then held his hand out towards her.

He thought she might refuse. They might have held hands on the way down, but they'd just both come out of a scary situation. He knew Alice hadn't really wanted anyone in NICU to know about them yet, but something had shifted between them.

She stood up and reached out and took his hand. There was no hesitation. And they walked back into the hospital and up to the unit together.

CHAPTER SEVEN

'WHY DIDN'T YOU tell me?' Penny had the widest smile on her face. It was the next day and it seemed that word had somehow leaked out about her and Dougie.

Alice shifted uncomfortably in the tiny coffee room on the unit. 'Because I wasn't sure if it was going to be something or not.'

'Well, it clearly is.' Penny hadn't stopped smiling.

Alice smiled too. 'Well, yes, maybe.'

Penny leaned against the wall and folded her arms. 'So, tell me more?'

Alice's phone sounded in her pocket and she pulled it out and frowned. Reading the message, she felt her stomach lurch.

'What's wrong?' Penny asked immediately, then pointed at the phone. 'And "King of Wishful Thinking" from *Pretty Woman* is far too easy to guess! And isn't it the nineties?'

Alice nodded automatically at her sister's guess. 'What can I say—I actually like that song. It's kind of catchy.'

'So, are you going to tell me what's wrong?' She should have known her sister wouldn't let it go. Penny was never easily brushed off.

'Promise me you won't flip.'

Penny's face was instantly worried. 'What do you mean?'

Alice sighed as she poured out two coffees. 'Okay, so remember when you moved away for a while?'

'With my disastrous ex-fiancé, yes.' Her brow furrowed. 'Why? What happened that you didn't tell me?'

Alice swallowed uncomfortably. She'd always known the day would come when she'd have to tell her sister what had happened. She never usually kept secrets from her sister and there had just never been a good time to bring this up.

'So, I met a guy on a dating app.'

'Not unusual,' said Penny, clearly wanting Alice to get to the point.

Alice sighed. 'I dated him for around six weeks—but then broke it off. I just got a bad vibe and decided he wasn't for me.'

'So what happened?' Penny's voice had

an edge to it. Alice knew she was going to be mad.

'Things got weird. He started turning up places I was. And things happened around the house.'

'What things?'

Alice pulled a face. 'My plant died.'

The furrows in Penny's brow deepened. 'The one at the front door?'

Alice nodded.

'But that's not so unusual.'

Alice sighed again. 'I know. But I bought a new one, and it died. And so did the third. Then I got a note pushed through the door, and a few messages from the same guy.'

'Who was he? Do I know him?'

Alice shook her head. 'I ended up speaking to George about him.'

'Our George?' It was clear Penny was surprised. Their friend George was a DC cop. He was steadfast and eminently sensible. But he wouldn't take crap from anyone.

Alice nodded. 'When I sat down and went over everything and asked for advice he told me it was stalking. He made me fill out an official report and went and had a chat with the guy. Things went quiet after that.'

'And you never told me any of this? Why not? How long did this go on for?'

Alice pushed a cup of coffee into her sister's hand in an effort to stop her waving it around. 'You had enough going on. You'd just found out Mitchel had a wife and kids. Last thing you needed was me giving you any more worries.'

Penny put her free hand on her chest. 'But I'm your sister. This is exactly the kind of stuff you should be telling me. You shouldn't have had to go through that yourself. Who was this guy, anyway?'

Alice shook her head. 'His name was Dave. He worked in IT. I think he probably wasn't well. But he'd misread just about everything between us. Said I'd led him on and encouraged him.'

'What?' Penny looked mad. But something else suddenly occurred to her. 'Idiot. So, what's happening now? Is that him that's just messaged you?'

Alice pulled out her phone and opened it with her fingerprint. 'He can't message me. I blocked him. But I've had some weird messages lately, through a few of the other dating apps.'

Penny swiped her screen. She turned to her sister. 'Where have they all gone?'

'The apps? Every time I get a weird message via one, I just delete it.'

'What kind of weird messages?'

Reuben, one of the doctors, came into the small space to grab a coffee. 'Excuse me,' he said, giving Alice a sideways glance that made her wonder if he'd heard part of their conversation. She waited until he'd left before continuing. She ran her fingers through her hair, untying her ponytail and tidying it up.

Penny pointed. 'You're anxious. You should have spoken to me about this sooner.'

'What?'

'You always do that, when you're anxious about something.' She gave a smile and lifted her eyebrows for a second. 'What's that word Dougie keeps using? Footering? That's what you're doing—footering with your hair.'

'Is that even a word? And I do not.' Alice shot a glare at her sister. She hated it when Penny was right.

'I'm your sister. I know. Now, tell me about these messages.'

Alice closed her eyes for a second. 'I have no idea who they are from—or if they are all from the same person. It's not like I haven't received a weird message before from a dating app. But all of the profiles have been recently formed, all with different photos. One was just quite obscene, so I deleted it and the app. Then another was just quite forward.

Naming a place they wanted to take me on a date, and what we could drink.'

'What was wrong with that?'

'The place they named was Roosters, and the drink was Sauvignon Blush.'

Penny's face was serious. 'Your regular bar for dates, and your regular drink?'

She nodded. 'I also got one that mentioned the top I was wearing that day and then another about the plant on my front doorstep.'

Penny put her hand on Alice's arm. 'You have to talk to George again. Have you told Dougie about this? What does he say?'

Alice rolled her eyes. 'No, I haven't told Dougie. This whole thing with him is brand-new. I don't want to tell him I've been registered on around seven different dating apps for the last year and things are catching up with me.'

Penny looked confused for a minute, then her jaw clenched. 'Stop it. You're not doing this. This is not your fault. Don't take the blame for this. You can be registered on as many different dating apps as you darn well please. It's no one's business but your own. And nothing is catching up with you. But this just doesn't seem right. Talking about what you're wearing and what's on your doorstep. That's just plain creepy.'

Hearing her sister say the words out loud let Alice focus. She'd been avoiding this, trying to brush it all off. The truth was, having Dougie in the house with her had made her feel safe. Protected. But that wasn't fair on him. This was her issue. She needed to deal with it herself.

'You're right,' she said. 'I'll talk to George again, and think about mentioning it to Dougie.' She raised a finger. 'But don't you do it. It's up to me.'

'Okay.' Penny nodded. 'But you better do it.' She stopped for a second and put her hands on Alice's shoulders. 'I wish you'd told me. I know I had other stuff happening, but you're still my sister, I still wanted to know.'

Alice's hand closed over her sister's. 'It worked out fine. I knew I needed help and George did that. And I don't want you to worry about any of this other stuff. Go and concentrate on Benedict and be happy.'

Penny looked at her sister again. 'Tell me if you need anything.' She glanced out of the coffee room to the NICU, where Dougie was talking to another doctor. 'And I want all the gossip on your new man.'

Alice took a final drink of coffee and rinsed out her mug, laughing at her sister. 'Absolutely not!'

As she walked out she felt a certain sense of relief that she'd finally filled her sister in on what had happened in the past. She cast her eyes over to where Dougie was standing. He was talking to the doctor who'd been assigned to their emergency delivery.

Alice made her way over. 'Any news on what's happening?'

The other guy, Kabir, gave a nod. 'Mom is in adult intensive care and hasn't regained consciousness yet. Her spleen and part of her liver were removed after the accident. She's had numerous transfusions, and her blood pressure has come up. From what I hear, they're considering reducing her sedation today.'

Dougie turned to face her. 'And our boy has a name. Lyle. Dad apparently was in last night, but is still really upset. Lyle is doing quite well. He's breathing on his own, with some additional oxygen, and although he was tube fed last night because he didn't have much motivation to suck, we're going to try again today.'

'Hello, Lyle.' Alice smiled as she looked down at the baby from yesterday. At thirty-three weeks he was bigger than a lot of the other babies in the unit. 'I'm glad to meet you properly. Yesterday was a big day.'

The nurse who had been looking after Lyle joined them. 'Dad was just in too much shock last night,' she said. 'But...' she smiled down at Lyle too '...hopefully when he comes back in today, we'll see if we can get him to hold you and try feeding you.'

'I'm on call tonight,' said Dougie. 'So, give me a shout if you need anything at all.'

Alice's heart gave a little lurch. 'You covering for someone?' She knew that Dougie wasn't due to be on call.

'Yeah, Lesley Jenkins is feeling under the weather. She asked if I would swap with her.' He glanced at Alice. 'We didn't have plans, did we?'

'No, not at all.' Except she would have liked to be honest with Dougie about the messages. She didn't think for a second he'd react badly. But it would have felt a little bit like a safety net if she'd told him.

She gave him a wave and made her way back to the twins, Ruby and Ryan. Both were doing okay right now. But Angie, their mum, just looked worse and worse.

Alice did all her normal checks on the babies, then sat down with Angie for a while. Angie admitted she hadn't been sleeping at all, and had no appetite. She was feeling guilty because the babies still seemed so detached from her, and she didn't feel like a real mom.

Alice understood. Everyone reacted differently to their baby being in NICU, and Angie had less support than some. She also said that the person she'd found easiest to talk to had been her labour and delivery nurse. It was normal for a patient to form an attachment to the person who'd been there for them during a traumatic time, and Alice wasn't at all upset to hear the person Angie had bonded with best wasn't her. This was about Angie. Alice had been doing this job long enough to know what was important. NICU often worked hand in hand with some of the midwifery or labour and delivery staff and after a quick chat Tara was able to negotiate some time for the nurse to come to the unit.

Things progressed quickly, with Angie agreeing to go out for a walk with the nurse and spend some time away from the unit—only on the proviso that Alice stayed with the babies.

As time moved on, Tara found her again. She gave a sad smile. 'So, Angie's scored highly on the postnatal depression scale, and has admitted to having an eating disorder. She's upset, but recognises she needs some support. The rest of the staff are working with her, but she's insisting you stay with her babies, otherwise she'll come back to the unit.' Tara held out her hands. 'You're due to finish soon and I don't want you to feel pressured into working extra hours if you have plans.'

Alice shook her head. 'I have no plans, and am happy to stay. If me being here is the reassurance that Angie needs, that's fine. I'm just glad she's opened up to someone and hopefully can start to get some help.'

Tara gave a small nod. 'Thanks, Alice.'

The hours passed slowly, but Alice didn't mind. There were other staff on duty in the NICU, but her being there as an extra meant that someone else wasn't assigned to the twins. They were perfect angels with no problems at all, making Alice's job easy.

Dougie was busy. There were a few new admissions and another baby who'd deteriorated and required intubation. There was a quiet hum to the unit for a couple of hours. Staff were efficient and Alice got a chance to sit back and watch for a while. She offered to help out on a few occasions, and to cover breaks, but being an extra pair of hands was odd to Alice and left her a bit restless.

Time was probably not what she needed right now. She had taken screenshots of the messages she'd received via the various apps. As she sat, she flicked through them and let her mind go backwards and forwards. One minute she'd decide they were all related to her previous stalker and things were serious. And then the next minute she decided that it was all just a series of unconnected unfortunate events.

The hours were starting to creep on, and Alice couldn't help how secretly glad she was not to be back at the house by herself. And it wasn't just about being unnerved. It was being around Dougie.

They might not be sitting together or talking, but she could feel his presence in the unit. She kept stealing little glances at him, the way his hair fell over his forehead, the expanse of his shoulders, how meticulous he was at work, when he looked serious, when he smiled and when he was joking with someone.

She was freaking herself out a little by how much she liked being around him and enjoyed his company. Wasn't this supposed to be how things went when you got together with someone?

Every now and then he caught her eye and gave her a smile. She could swear it was only for her.

He was relatively easygoing at home. They'd made a rule not to talk about work, but there was a whole host of other things to talk about. They'd planned some more day trips. He was happy to go for a walk with her around the city, meandering around a few stores, buying a takeout coffee and just wasting a few hours together. Movie marathons were a must, usually followed by an impassioned argument about best/worst movie, character, actor, setting, prop, or a mixture of them all.

She should be happy. She should be over the moon. But still the restlessness was there, the tiny doubts. She didn't know if the spate of messages had just unsettled her again—reminding her not to let down her guard and that appearances could be deceptive.

She looked up as he gave her a wave and made her way over. He was sitting next to Lyle's incubator, and what she hadn't noticed at first was that he had Lyle tucked into the crook of his neck.

She kept her voice to a whisper as she sat down in the chair next to him, before glancing around and putting her tired feet up on another chair. She edged her chair around so she still had a clear view of the twins' monitors. 'What are you doing?'

Dougie shrugged. 'Dad came in. But he only lasted a few minutes holding Lyle. It's all too much for him. He has a two-year-old daughter who keeps asking for her momma and his wife is still sedated in ICU, and the guy was literally just in pieces. I sent him back to ICU because it's clear that's where he needs to be right now.'

'So how come you've got Lyle?'

Dougie smiled down at the little figure, who seemed entirely comfortable. Lyle's face was close to Dougie's neck and his body was resting near the top of his chest over the thin scrubs that he was wearing. Dougie's scrubs meant that the baby had access to some parts of his skin, and one little hand was placed at the bottom of Dougie's throat.

'This little guy decided not to settle after his father held him. I think he liked the human contact. He's been wailing since then, so I decided it was time for a rest break for me and I'd have it holding him.'

'You're supposed to be on a break?'

He nodded but patted Lyle's back. 'This is a break. He's settled. He's happy. He managed to take some milk earlier; his sucking reflex is good.'

'Fabulous.' Alice smiled. It was one of the key steps for any baby who came into NICU.

Sucking and being able to feed was such a crucial skill, and some babies were born too early for that mechanism to have kicked in. But Lyle was thirty-three weeks. He was right on the cusp of being able to suck, and it was good news for him.

Alice shook her head as she rested back in the chair. How could she harbour doubts about a guy like this? Her skin prickled. This was about her. She had to make the step to trust again. She had to stop looking for something, anything, to give her an excuse not to.

'How's Ruby and Ryan?'

She gave a nod; it was a welcome distraction from her own thoughts. 'Really good. Observations stable. Oxygen levels good. No apparent digestion problems so far. They've been perfect tonight.'

She couldn't help but notice how tender he was being with Lyle. Every now and then he tilted his chin downwards and whispered to the little guy while rubbing his back gently.

He could see her watching him. 'You know what I find most fascinating?' he said in a low voice.

'What?'

'How every baby likes to be held differently. I've worked with some real old school staff who maintained there was only one way to hold a baby and they had the precious answer that worked for every baby. And the best of that was—they all said something different.'

Alice smiled and nodded in agreement. 'I've met some of them.'

Dougie lifted his free hand. 'Well, *they* might have had a preferred way to hold a baby. But it doesn't work for every baby. I had this little one every which way. I do believe in skin to skin. But that's primarily for the parent or carer. But isn't it interesting that Lyle has settled best when part of his skin can touch mine—even if it's only a tiny part? And I can feel every breath whilst he's against the top of my chest, just like he can sense mine.'

'You like this, don't you?'

'Doesn't everyone who works in a NICU?'

He had a point. Most staff who worked here were happy to take the time to settle a restless or uncomfortable baby, or to help a parent do the same. There was nothing nicer than seeing a baby sleeping, with their little chest going steadily up and down after a period of unrest.

But what Alice was having most trouble with was watching Dougie up close and personal with a baby. The care. The affection. It was written all over him and it was a side to him she'd never seen before.

She'd known he was a good and competent doctor. She'd known he was particular, with exacting standards. But this was new.

'Have you got young kids in your family?'

He looked at her in surprise. 'No, I'm an only child. But lots of the people I went through medical school with have settled down and have kids. Some of my friends from previous jobs too. I'm godfather to a good friend in Scotland's daughter. She's fourteen now, though, and keeps trying to make me do those fifteen-second dance clips.'

'And you say no?'

'I do the world a favour by saying no, believe me. Anyhow, any time there's any kind of reunion I always end up holding someone's baby, or entertaining the two-year-olds.' He grinned. 'Haven't you found that? Because you work in NICU, other folks think you'll be a natural with children. Then you find yourself surrounded by two-year-olds who seem like giants. Or babies born at a normal gestation and everyone questions you about weaning, or crawling, or immunisations at fifteen months.' He started to laugh. 'And then you want to hold your hands up and say, That's *way* past my area of expertise.'

Alice laughed too. 'We could probably have a competition called *What's That Rash?* How many times have you been sent a photo on your phone saying, Is this meningitis, measles, chickenpox, foot and mouth…?'

Dougie joined in. 'Prickly heat, slapped cheek, ringworm, scarlet fever, hives…' He raised his eyebrows. 'You've got all those photos too.'

She shifted her feet from the chair. 'We could probably write a book.'

'Would it stop the calls or texts?'

'Probably not.'

'Then what's the point?'

'True.' She stood up. 'I'm going back to my little angels. I expect Angie will be back some time soon.'

'Here's hoping she's going to start feeling better soon.'

'I'll let you know how it goes.' She went to move away, but Dougie stopped her.

'Alice?'

She spun back around. 'Yeah?'

'People know about us now.' His voice was steady, but there was a slight question in his tone.

She licked her lips and nodded.

'And you're okay with that?'

'Are you?' Her stomach clenched, wondering if he might not say what she expected.

He shrugged. 'Of course. Just don't want you feeling uncomfortable at work. You've known these people longer than me.' For just a second, she thought she heard a hint of anxiety in his voice. Something that didn't seem like him. The familiar wave of *Do you know him at all?* swept over her. But she was determined to at least try and push past it.

She pasted a smile on her face. 'Prepare yourself. There might be questions asked. I've never dated anyone from work before.'

'Ah…they'll want to know what my secret is?'

'Maybe.' She shrugged as she walked away.

She kept the smile on her face until she reached the twins again. It was perfect timing; they were due their observations recorded again, and both would likely need their diapers changed.

She washed her hands and glanced at the clock. It was close to eleven. She wasn't quite sure she fancied going home alone on the Metro. Part of her didn't even want Angie to come back because it gave her an excuse to stay longer. But she was sensible enough to realise that she couldn't continue to function as a nurse for any longer. It didn't matter that her area of responsibility was much more reduced than normal. She doted on these twins, and wanted to be alert and on the ball if there was even a minuscule deterioration in their condition. They had been great for the whole day, but Alice had worked in NICU too long to take anything for granted.

Just at that the doors hissed open and Angie walked in, the labour and delivery nurse still by her side. They both looked tired, but there was something different on Angie's face, a relaxation that hadn't been there before.

'I'm so sorry, I was away so long, Alice,' she said.

Alice shook her head. 'It's no problem at all. You'll be pleased to know that Ruby and Ryan are doing fine. How about you?'

Angie glanced at Indira, the labour and delivery nurse, who gave her the tiniest nod. Angie took a deep breath. 'Can you tell me who will be on duty for the rest of the night? I know you need to go home and get some rest.'

One of their colleagues, Matt, came over. 'I'm on duty tonight. Ruby and Ryan will be with me.'

Alice sent a silent prayer upwards. She knew that Angie liked Matt just as much as she liked herself.

Angie nodded. 'In that case, would you mind if I went home and caught up on some sleep, and come back in tomorrow morning? Indira has arranged a cab for me.'

It was a first. And it was huge. They all knew it. Making the decision to trust the staff and to take some time out for herself was such a positive choice for Angie to make.

Matt gave her a broad smile. 'You know you can trust me, Angie. If I was worried about anything I would call you. But it looks like Ruby and Ryan are settled, and I hope that's how they will remain all night. Get some sleep, and you can see them in the morning.'

Angie nodded again, as if she was reassuring herself on the decision she had made. 'You will phone me?' she asked.

'One hundred per cent,' said Matt.

They stepped back and gave Angie a chance to say goodnight to her babies.

'Well done,' whispered Alice to Indira.

'First steps,' Indira whispered back. 'There's a lot to unpick and this will be a journey. But she's finally starting to acknowledge that she has to look at her own health and wellbeing too.'

Once Angie had left, Matt put a hand on

Alice's shoulder. 'You too, girl. Hate to say it, but you look tired.'

'I feel tired,' she admitted. 'I was just about to come find you. Just not sure about going home this late at night on the subway.'

He glanced at his watch. 'Think you might just have missed the last one.'

'Darn it.' Her heart sank. She wasn't keen on the idea of a cab and there weren't exactly many comfortable sleeping options around the hospital for her.

'Hey.' Dougie appeared at her side and slid his arm around her shoulders. In his other hand he held out a key. 'Sleep in the on-call room. I'm likely to be up most of the night anyhow.'

Matt tried to hide his smile as he stepped away to deal with Ruby and Ryan.

She met Dougie's gaze. Those blue eyes had a smile in them. He was half teasing her, wondering if she would accept. Knowing it would send a further message to their colleagues. But, instead of being worried at all, it was like wrapping a warm blanket around her heart.

She'd never felt like this before. This was the kind of thing that Penny had tried to get her to understand. The pure elation of being in a relationship with someone you felt deeply for—maybe even loved?

The thought made heat rush into her cheeks and she reached out and grabbed the key. 'Thanks,' she said, her voice steady and sure. Because she wanted to be sure. Sure that this was the right move for her and for her Scotsman.

There were still things to learn about each other. But wasn't that part of the nature of a relationship, anyway? No one got to know someone instantly. There would always be learning, always be growth. She would tell him about her past stalking experience. Maybe he would tell her what was going on when he got that occasionally haunted look in his eyes.

She leaned into him, letting herself press up against the length of his body. 'I'm going to jump in the staff showers and find a new pair of scrubs to sleep in and steal one of the emergency toothbrushes.' She gave him a wink. 'If it's not too busy overnight, I might shift over a little and let you in the tiny bed they have in these on-call rooms.'

'How do you know how small the beds are?' His eyebrows were slightly raised.

'Let's just say that on more than one occasion I've had to wake up a junior that's slept through his page.'

Dougie nodded. 'Been guilty of that a few times in the past.'

He moved and then stopped, and she smiled. Because she knew exactly what he'd been about to do. He'd been about to drop a kiss on her forehead. But work was not the place for that.

A little part inside her was singing, that he felt so comfortable around her that he'd momentarily forgotten where they were.

'See you soon,' he said in a low voice, with a look in his eyes that made her practically skip all the way to the shower and try, once again, to make the effort to trust someone.

It was official. He was part of a couple. It seemed that everyone in the entire hospital knew and Dougie kept getting the odd nod or smile from people he didn't know. When he got to the hospital canteen, he could sense a few nudges and glances from colleagues. And if he and Alice hit the canteen together, he could sense eyes on them everywhere.

Not that he minded as such. Hospitals like this were so big that news was only really news for a short while before it faded, to be replaced by the next thing that people were talking about.

Alice's friend from Spain, Mariela, had put in her official notice as her mother was going to need extensive rehab. Tara had already interviewed and the new member of staff was due to start in the next few days.

Dougie was trying his best to avoid the temptation of overseeing everyone else's work in the unit. The staff were proving capable and competent. One of the more junior doctors had come to speak to him about calculations around doses for one of the medicines, and Dougie had been relieved that the guy had asked rather than just carry on himself. It turned out that the other doctor had done everything completely correctly—but, because it was his first time, wanted to check with someone more senior before writing the prescription and delivering the doses. Next time Dougie saw him he'd had a tiny laminated chart made and slipped it into the pocket of his wallet so he could check again in future.

It was completely understandable. The doctor's last position had been in an adult ward and the doses for these premature babies were minuscule in comparison.

He admired the easy way Alice was at

work. Although her actions were precise, her manner with patients and all those around her seemed completely relaxed. She teased him about being uptight, and occasionally rubbed his shoulders on the way past.

They'd had dinner in the past few weeks with her sister, Penny, and her fiancé, Benedict. Since Benedict was partly his boss, Dougie had wondered if it might be a little awkward, but Benedict was great, interested in the places he'd worked and some of the procedures in place in other hospitals. Although Dougie had mentioned the London hospital he'd worked in before Washington, it clearly didn't ring any alarm bells for Benedict, and Dougie had been silently relieved.

Kayla's previous workplaces had been detailed throughout her trial, with mentions of the suspicions raised by another doctor—him. It might only have been in a few newspapers, but he hated the fact that if someone did an internet search for Kayla's name, and his, they were both connected for eternity, along with the fact they had 'dated'. But Benedict didn't even blink when Dougie mentioned his previous workplace.

It turned out they had a mutual colleague who was now working in Australia but was hoping to come back to Washington soon, and it was likely there would be a vacancy due to a retirement in the unit soon. Penny and Alice meantime had been busy talking about plans for Penny and Benedict's upcoming wedding.

Benedict and Penny were also staunch fans of the ringtone game, and when Benedict's phone had started playing Starship's 'Nothing's Gonna Stop Us Now' there had been a few seconds of silence around the table before Dougie, Alice and Penny had all simultaneously shouted, *'Mannequin!'*

Things in the townhouse had heated up accordingly, with them sometimes spending the night in Alice's bed, and sometimes spending the night in Dougie's. He'd noticed that occasionally she seemed on edge, but any time he asked she just shook it off and said nothing was wrong.

It left him slightly uneasy. Nothing about Alice was wrong. She was intelligent, funny, definitely smart-mouthed, gorgeous and a great nurse. But every time he felt as if she was keeping something from him he had flashbacks to London. It didn't matter he'd gone out with Kayla on one date. His radar had been off. He hadn't listened to his gut. Was he doing the same here?

Dougie hated that his thoughts went that

way. Alice had done absolutely nothing wrong. He was also conscious that it was more himself he hated, because he still felt as if he should have raised the red flag earlier about Kayla. In some ways, she and Alice were similar—bright, friendly and easy to be around. But that was where the similarities ended. Alice was passionate about the care she delivered to her patients. She was meticulous. Her recording was excellent. Even when practice didn't dictate it, she regularly asked another member of staff to double-check a medicine before she administered it. Kayla had been all gloss on the surface with none of the good practice underneath.

Dougie walked over to the nearest window as he waited for the timer on the oven to sound. Alice was due in from her yoga class at any minute and he had simple oat and raisin cookies in the oven, along with *Raiders of the Lost Ark* lined up on the TV.

He heard her key in the lock and she came in, chatting on the phone to one of her friends. She gave him a wave, then bent down to pick up something lying on the mat at her feet.

She stopped moving for a moment, then stuffed it into her bag, her face pale. As she cut her call, she noticed he was watching her.

'What was that?'

'Nothing.' She waved her hand. 'Just a flyer about an event. I'm going to go upstairs and jump in the shower. Okay?'

He nodded, but it was as if a gust of wind prickled the hairs at the back of his neck.

The alarm sounded and he slid the cookies from the oven, his appetite completely gone. He knew she hadn't been truthful with him. In the UK, everyone had a letterbox on their door, meaning just about anything could be posted through it. But here in the US most people around had a mailbox in front of their house, or a central point where mail was delivered. If someone had stuffed a flyer on the doorframe he would have noticed when he got home earlier. It must just have happened. His mouth was dry. Alice wouldn't get upset about a flyer. But it was clear she wasn't ready to share what was wrong. He started up the stairs to talk to her. The shower was running, but he could hear her on the phone again, even though she'd finished her call downstairs.

He heard the word 'Penny' and turned and left. The last thing he was going to do was listen in to a phone call between sisters. It wasn't his style, and it wasn't his business. He took himself back down the stairs to wait, putting the cookies onto a plate and pouring chilled wine into two glasses.

When Alice came back down the stairs fifteen minutes later, her roughly dried hair was up in a ponytail and she'd put on her pyjamas. The outside edges of her eyes were ever so slightly red. But if he hadn't witnessed her reaction to whatever had been left at the door he would never have noticed.

She smiled when she saw the cookies, the wine and the waiting movie on the screen. 'What more could a girl ask for?' she said as she made her way over to the sofa.

He didn't want to ask more questions. He didn't want to be invasive. It was clear that she wanted him here. As she snuggled up alongside him, he could smell her orange-scented shampoo. It washed over him in a familiar way.

He liked it. No. He didn't just like it. He didn't just *like* Alice Greene. He was losing his heart to Alice Greene. Every turn of her head, every quip, every wink and every smile made his heartbeat quicken just a little more. When she turned over in the dead of night and flung one leg and arm over him, he didn't wriggle out from under her. He just laughed and pulled her closer. Alice Greene was well and truly under his skin.

He hadn't come here looking for love. He'd come to Washington as a means of escape. A way to start somewhere new, and a place where he could start to have confidence in his judgement again. He could have ended up anywhere. There had been jobs in Boston, New York, Florida, Hawaii, New Zealand and Australia. This had almost been a random pick. Only the pull of the reputation of the NICU and its staff had brought him here.

Dating had been the last thing on his mind. Love had absolutely been the last thing on his mind. But someone, somewhere had flipped a dime and landed him in the NICU at the exact time when Alice had a space to fill in her home. He'd only been supposed to be here for a week and it was coming up to two months.

He'd never been this settled before—not even when he was home in Scotland. He was beginning to understand the old words, *Home is where the heart is*. And Dougie MacLachlan's heart was in Washington. Whether he'd said it out loud or not.

He pushed all the tiny doubts that niggled him out of his mind.

He put one arm around her shoulders and hugged her closer. Alice made a little noise and put her head halfway on his shoulder and halfway on his chest.

She was munching one of his cookies.

'You know and I know that all those cookie crumbs are going to end up on me instead of you.'

'I guess you need to learn how to make crumb-less cookies.' She sighed. 'I blame the baker.'

'Well, I guess I blame the baker too. Hey, am I still on a trial?' he joked.

'Oh, that boat sailed a long time ago,' she said, then paused for a second and added, 'I don't think I ever told you the trial was over, did I?'

'You did not. That's why I'm still baking. I think I'm still on probation and I'm trying to impress. It's exhausting,' he joked. 'Between that and keeping up with the laundry and cleaning, I'm just about ready to collapse in a heap.'

She turned around onto her back, her head across his lap, and looked up at him. She had a soft smile on her face, but her dark eyes were serious. 'Well, let's just settle this now. Dougie, are you going to stay?'

The question came from left field. But he didn't hesitate in his response because it came from the heart. 'I want to.' He paused for a moment, then asked the question he knew he should. Because he still knew that, deep down, she was hiding something from him. 'Do you want me to?'

She smiled and wound her hands up around his neck, giving a nod towards the TV. 'See that girl in the movie?'

He looked up in time to see Indiana Jones deliver a lecture to his pupils, where one girl was blinking at him. She had 'LOVE YOU' written on her eyelids. He looked back down and put one hand on Alice's stomach. 'Yeah?'

She gave him a big smile. 'Well, that's me. I'm that girl.'

He couldn't even describe the warm sensation that spread over him. He leaned down to kiss her. 'Is that a yes then?' His smile matched hers.

His lips were only millimetres from hers. He could feel her warm breath on his skin, mixing with the smell of soap from her skin. 'That's definitely a yes,' she whispered as her lips met his.

Her hands ran through his hair as they continued to kiss, and his lips moved from her face, to her neck. 'I just want you to know,' he said between kisses, 'that if you were the professor, I'd be the student with "LOVE YOU" on my eyelids.'

Her grin was wider than he could have hoped for. 'You would?' she breathed as he kept kissing the soft skin around her neck.

'Definitely.'

And from that point onwards *Raiders of the Lost Ark* was forgotten.

CHAPTER EIGHT

IT WAS LIKE being in a happy bubble. Alice
had always thought she led a happy life. She'd
grown up with two loving parents and a fan-
tastic older sister. The Army life had meant
that she'd learned how to be adaptable, moving bases every few years, living in different countries and cultures and making new
friends.

As an adult, she could see now how that
upbringing had shaped her for nursing. She
absolutely understood how communication
was such a key part of relationships and her
working life, so why hadn't she yet let Dougie
know that something was wrong in her life?

It was simple. She didn't want the happy
bubble to burst.

She was enjoying waking up next to the
sometimes grumpy Scotsman. She enjoyed
sharing her home with him. Exploring Washington with him had made the whole city fun

again for her. She was going back to places she'd visited when she'd first arrived here and never visited again since.

She loved this city. Sure, lots of people moved away from the city centre when they wanted to get married and have a family. But Benedict and Penny had found the perfect place to live, and they planned to bring up a family. There was no reason that Washington couldn't be a for ever home.

She pulled her phone from her pocket and sighed. The flyer last week had really thrown her. All it had said was:

Carol
Yoga Class 7-8 p.m. Tuesdays
Westgrove Center

To anyone else it would simply look like a flyer for a class. But it wasn't that. It was a message. At least that was what Alice thought it was. A message saying that whoever was watching her knew that she went to class every Tuesday night. She'd thought she might be sick and had run up the stairs to speak to Penny. Thank goodness she'd told her sister now, because Penny had talked her down. She'd made Alice take a breath and not panic. Yes, she agreed, it was scary, but it could also be coincidence. And until they knew any different she should keep calm. Dougie was there in the meantime, and Penny had encouraged her to tell him.

She'd wanted to. She was going to tell him when she got back downstairs. But as soon as she'd looked at his face her whole heart had just squeezed. She didn't want Dougie to think about the possibility of his girlfriend being stalked. Part of her still wondered if he'd think she'd encouraged this stranger in any way. But their relationship was evolving every day, and she wanted to keep it like that.

Alice had never truly been serious about anyone before. Things had never lasted more than a few months. They'd either fizzled out naturally or she'd called a halt because she knew she wasn't feeling it. Ever since the stalker incident, she hadn't been able to trust her own judgement. This was the first time she had. *Felt it*. And even though she had a completely adult and rational brain, right now she didn't want anything to destroy her bubble.

But it wasn't just that. There was still something about Dougie she couldn't put her finger on. It was never at home—always at work. Some staff had made remarks that his checks irritated them or made them feel as if they were under the microscope. Another experienced practitioner had given him a curt dismissal when he'd double-checked something with her. All of them now knew that Alice and Dougie were dating. So she was sure if he were annoying her colleagues, most of them wouldn't let her in on the chat. But she just knew there was something else going on. Something else that was making him cautious at work. She wished he'd tell her what it was, but the irony of that struck her hard. They were both keeping secrets from each other. He might be doing what she was right now—wanting to actually talk about it, but just not sure when the right time would be.

Her phone sounded again. An unknown number.

'Hello?'

There was some weird crackling, as if the line hadn't quite connected or there was static somewhere.

'Hello?' she tried again. But there still wasn't anything she could hear properly. After a few moments Alice cut the call. But it left her feeling distinctly uncomfortable. With everything else that had gone on, she hated the thought that someone creepy might have her number. The dating apps didn't give out personal emails or phone numbers. All messaging had to be done via the apps—it was how they made their money.

It was nothing. It was just someone dialling the wrong number by mistake.

She shook off her doubts and got ready for work. Dougie had left earlier but she was doing a favour for a colleague and covering part of their shift so they could take their teenage kid to a recital.

It didn't take long to take the subway into work. Angie was sitting beside the twins and was looking excited. 'Perfect!' she said as Alice strolled in. 'They said I could get to hold them for a while today. I asked if you'd be in, and they said you were in at lunchtime.'

It was honestly the first time that Alice had seen a genuine smile on Angie's face, and it swamped her with relief that she might be turning a corner. She glanced up at Alice. 'Would you mind calling Indira? I'd really like it if she was here too.'

'Absolutely no problem at all. Give me five minutes and I'll be right back,' said Alice as she made her way over to the nurses' station.

Dougie was talking to another doctor, and Tara turned to greet her. 'Oh, hi, Alice. Say hello to our new colleague, Jake. He worked at the NICU in St Gabriel's in London.'

'That's where Dougie worked,' Alice said automatically. 'Did you two know each other?'

She held out her hand to shake the tall black man's hand. Dougie's head shot around. He looked at the new nurse. He gave a minimal shake of his head and also held out his hand.

Jake shook both. 'No, sorry,' he said. 'You must have worked there before me.'

Alice could swear Dougie looked relieved. His smile was broad, but a little forced. 'Did you work with Charles Edwards?'

Jake nodded. 'Loved working with him. His enthusiasm is infectious.'

'Absolutely.'

'Sorry,' said Jake, 'tell me your name again. I'm getting lost in the sea of new names today.'

'Dougie.' He paused, then added his surname. 'Dougie MacLachlan.'

Something flitted across Jake's face. 'Oh, nice to meet you.'

Tara leaned forward. 'Jake's going to be shadowing for his first few days, so he'll be with Lynn for a few hours and then with you, Alice. That okay?'

Alice gave Jake a smile. 'Sure, just come and find me. I'm at Bays Eleven and Twelve, Twenty-Three and Twenty-Four.'

She made the call to Indira, then spent the

next few hours watching the pleasure on Angie's face as she got to hold first Ruby and then Ryan. They took lots of photos and encouraged her to just let the babies lie on her skin and rest for a few hours.

Her phone sounded again. Another unknown number, with no real person at the end of the call. Alice ducked into the changing rooms and tried to call George, her friend who was a cop, for some advice. But George didn't answer. After pausing for a few moments she left a message, asking if he could call her back some time. She hated the fact she might be wasting his time.

By the time she finished work it was getting dark. It was only ten o'clock, but Dougie was still caught up with a patient. 'You go on, I'll catch up with you later.'

She was ready to make an excuse, say something so she could just wait for him too. But she was tired and her back was sore. She actually wanted to go home and soak in the bath for an hour and then hopefully be relaxed enough to sit and enjoy some time with Dougie later.

She was fed up with being afraid of something that likely wasn't real. This was *her* city. Her place. She'd gone home alone over a hundred times. She'd travelled the subway at night dozens of times. Why was she even hesitating? Alice picked up her backpack and gave Dougie a wave. 'See you later.'

She changed quickly and caught the line to Foggy Bottom. The subway wasn't busy. She noticed the odd person who was clearly going home from work like herself. A few couples and some groups of friends.

It was dark by the time she emerged from the subway, but the road to the townhouse was clearly lit. It was a warm, muggy kind of evening. Other nights had been slightly colder, but Alice took off her zip-up top and tied it around her waist as she walked home.

She'd been listening to an audio book for the entirety of the journey home. She liked crime thrillers best to listen to, as they seemed to hold her attention better. She turned off the main street, which had been relatively busy, and onto her own road, which was much quieter. There were a few lights at windows and she admired other people's window boxes or potted plants or ferns as she strolled along.

She was so lost in her book that she wasn't really paying much attention to anything else. So as she reached her door she fumbled for her key and dropped it on the ground.

The shove crashed her head into her own front door.

Alice fell to her knees, trying to make sense of what had just happened.

One hand tightened around her backpack and she waited for the tug at her shoulders. She'd never been mugged before, but she expected that was what was happening now.

But the tug never came. Instead, a pair of dark sneakers came into her vision as a force lifted her back up onto her feet. Her key was still somewhere on the ground beneath her.

Alice's immediate thought was to get away. She started struggling, lashing out and kicking. Years before, she'd been taught breakaway training as part of her nurse training, but because she worked in the NICU she hadn't gone to an update for a few years and it hadn't felt like an immediate issue. Right now, she was wishing she'd attended.

There was a yelp from whoever was trying to restrain her, but next thing she was slammed back against the door, with hands at her throat.

Her phone started to ring, but she had no way to get to it. Both of her hands were at her neck, trying to release the clamping feeling at her throat.

Her eyes were wide and a face hissed up

next to her. 'Leading someone else on now, Alice?'

Dread flooded through her. She recognised that voice. Dave. The guy who had stalked her. The one who had to be warned off.

'Saw you on the dating apps again. Why didn't you reply to my messages?'

He was hissing up next to her ear. She could feel flecks of his saliva landing on her. But she just couldn't breathe. She tried to form words.

'L-let g-go…'

His hands released her neck slightly.

'You've…been…following me…phoning me,' she said.

Her brain was going crazy. Penny would have no idea she was in trouble. She hadn't managed to get hold of George. Dougie was still at the hospital. She frantically looked at the other windows in the street. Some homes had their blinds closed. Some were completely dark—as if the residents weren't home at all. Others had lights on, but no one was looking out of their window right now. There was no one to help her.

'Thought you might have learned from last time. Thought you might have stopped leading men on. But that hasn't happened, has it?'

Dave sounded angry, bitter. It had been over

two years since they'd dated. She couldn't believe this was happening. She should have made the call to George earlier. She should have trusted her instinct. And she should have told Dougie.

But all that was too late now. Anger surged through her. How dare this guy do this to her?

'Get off me!' she spat.

She lifted one elbow and caught the side of his face. His grip loosened slightly and she took full advantage. She bent double—something he clearly wasn't expecting her to do. But her change of position made his weight adjust. Alice was ignoring the fact that deliberately leaning into the strangle was killing her. She whipped her body back up and caught him under the chin with the back of her head.

She was sure that anyone would tell this was a terrible move—and that she would likely cause more injury to herself than to him. But while she was momentarily stunned Dave had let go and he staggered backwards. Adrenaline was rushing through her now.

'Alice!' The voice came from down the street and she could hear thudding footsteps coming towards her. But her blood was racing now, and she wasn't done yet. Dave started to straighten; he had pure venom in his face towards her. She didn't hesitate. Not for a second. She lifted her foot and kicked him square in the balls. The move that every teenage girl had been taught by her older sister or cheerleader colleagues as an emergency move.

The yelp echoed around her. She sagged back against the door, conscious that right now she should be grabbing her key and getting behind a closed door, and safety. But those footsteps were almost at her. Dougie launched himself through the air as if he was playing a game of American football and took the guy clean down. There was a short tussle. But Dave was no match for Dougie's muscles, physique or pure Scottish rage. He held the guy down, with one arm pinning him to the ground. Alice was conscious of the fact that moments earlier it had been Dave's hand around her throat.

'Keep him down,' she said with a croaky voice. 'But don't hurt him.'

Dougie changed position as Alice fumbled for her phone. She redialled George.

'Who is this guy?' asked Dougie.

'An ex. One who stalked me and was warned off.'

Her call connected and George's calm

voice came on the line. 'Hey, Alice. You okay? What do you need?'

'Help,' she said swiftly. 'I've just been attacked by the guy that stalked me.'

The tone of George's voice changed immediately. 'Where are you?'

'At my front door.'

'Are you safe right now?'

She looked at Dave, pinned on the ground beneath Dougie. He wasn't going anywhere. 'Yes.'

'I'm on my way. I've put a call out for the nearest unit.'

She looked at Dougie. 'Police are on their way.'

Dave started cursing and wriggling under Dougie's grip.

'Don't make me punch you. You've no idea how much I want to right now,' said Dougie, his accent the thickest she'd ever heard it. Something about it seemed to still Dave. Maybe he was having flashbacks to the characters in *Trainspotting*.

Her hands went to her throat. Even though she was free, the feeling of constriction was still there. She started coughing, knowing it was likely a psychological reaction to the event.

'Alice, are you okay?'

She nodded although she was coughing. 'I just need something to drink. Wait until the cops get here.'

Dougie looked down at the guy underneath him in disgust. 'He was stalking you?' His voice was incredulous. 'Why on earth didn't you tell me?'

She felt tears well in her eyes. But the anger was still there. The anger about everything falling down around about her.

'Now's not the time,' she said. She wasn't even sure where to start.

Dougie stayed where he was, keeping Dave away from her until the police arrived, closely followed by George. Everything happened in a blur. She was asked to go downtown and give a statement. When she called Penny to let her know what had happened, Penny was distraught and insisted on coming to meet her. When she was finally finished at the police station, Penny, Benedict and Dougie had all noticed her persistent cough and insisted she get checked out by one of their colleagues.

The last thing Alice wanted to do was end up in the ER and become the latest gossip, but one of the doctors she knew examined her in a side room. By then, purple bruising had spread across her throat and they all knew what he would say. Her voice was hoarse and the cough annoying. 'You've got definite soft tissue damage. I'd like to keep you in for observation.'

She shook her head.

'There are risks attached to attempted strangulation. Not all injuries are evident straight away. You could have some difficulty breathing if the swelling continues. I need to know straight away if you have problems swallowing, or you have any further voice changes. Headaches or light-headedness are also issues.'

'You should stay,' Penny said automatically. 'Or come home with me.'

Alice wasn't sure how to answer. Dougie would be at her place. But she wasn't sure she could face seeing her own front door right now. Even imagining it in her head was giving her flashbacks.

'Go with Penny and Benedict,' Dougie agreed, and her stomach dropped. He wanted rid of her. He didn't want to be around her.

Penny's face lit up with relief and she wrapped an arm around Alice's shoulders. 'Absolutely. We can sleep in the spare room together. I'll keep an eye on you, and if we need to get back to the hospital quickly we can do that.'

Alice was blinking back tears. 'We're not kids any more, Penny.' She couldn't help but be slightly embarrassed by her older sister.

'When someone's hurt my sister—you better believe I move into big sister mode. I'm in beside you tonight. I'll notice if you start wheezing or anything.' She squeezed Alice again and set off another coughing fit. 'Oh, no, sorry…sorry.'

Alice shook her head. Dougie had already stood up; he looked very awkward. There was only one thing she could read for definite from him right now—he wanted to get away.

He turned back and reached out and touched her shoulder. 'Do you need me to get you anything?'

Penny answered for her. 'No, we're the same size. She can wear my things. And I have everything else that she needs.'

'Great. Okay then. Give me a text if there's anything you think of.'

The silence was painful. At least it was to Alice. She wasn't sure that Penny or Benedict noticed. So she just gave a nod.

Dougie locked eyes with her for a few seconds and she caught the confusion and hurt that lingered there. She wanted to reach out and grab him. Tell him to stay and say they could talk. But she honestly didn't feel up to it. She was traumatised. She was exhausted. And all she wanted to do right now was sleep. Maybe for a month. So she just licked her lips, gave him a weak smile and watched him walk away.

CHAPTER NINE

DOUGIE WASN'T QUITE sure what was happening in his life. The person he loved, lived with and slept with had been attacked. He couldn't get the sight out of his head. Every time he closed his eyes he saw Alice pinned to her door, her face red and a look of absolute terror on her face.

What would have happened if he had been five minutes later? The doors had been sliding on the subway as he'd jumped to get in. If they'd slid closed and he'd missed it?

He couldn't bear it. But these were the thoughts that were constantly swimming around in his head. He'd spent the last two nights at home in the townhouse. It was odd without Alice. Sooty definitely missed her, and as soon as he had entered each day the cat was practically attached to his leg.

But the overwhelming thing for Dougie was the fact she hadn't told him. Someone had been stalking his girlfriend—and she had chosen not to share. What did that say about him? Part of him wondered if Alice had realised he hadn't been totally honest himself, and that had made her reluctant to share with him. If that was the reason, then all of this was entirely his fault.

If she'd shared, he would never have let her go home alone. They could have set up some kind of alert system—anything that might have made her safer. He didn't understand the bond between sisters—because he had no siblings. But he'd seen the look of horror on Penny's face. That was why he'd suggested Alice go back home with her. He'd known that Penny would never have settled without being near her sister. And he didn't want to get in the way of that. He wasn't even sure how Alice might feel about the townhouse now. It was beautiful, a gorgeous home, but would it now be associated with bad memories for Alice?

There was something else too. That little wave of anger that lingered. He was angry with Alice. Angry that she hadn't told him. Every cell in his body told him how inappropriate that was—particularly in his own set of circumstances. But trust felt like the underlying issue here. If she didn't trust him, what else was there?

There had barely been a few texts between them. He'd sent the obligatory How are you feeling? the next day. But the response had been short.

Will be better in a few days.

He wasn't even sure how to read that. Did she want him to visit? Was that a request to give her a bit of space?

He'd been working on autopilot these last two days and that made him mad at himself. As he changed to go into the unit today, he was determined to be back to normal.

The unit was busy. There had been four new admissions overnight. Benedict had been on duty and it was clear from one look that he hadn't got a wink of sleep.

Dougie walked over quickly. 'Give me a handover and go home. You look knackered.'

Benedict smiled at the Scottish word. 'Alice has picked up your words. She called me crabbit the other day.'

Dougie couldn't help the smile. 'How was she last night?'

'Insisting she's coming back to work today.'

'What?'

Benedict took a deep breath. 'I know, I know. Penny kept telling her not to. But she's apparently made an arrangement with Tara to do a half-shift today. Feel free to tell her to go home too.'

Dougie wasn't quite sure what to say. 'I'll talk to her later. Now, give me a handover.'

The handover took much longer than normal. The four babies admitted overnight all had complications; a few were on complicated drug regimes. Two other babies in the unit had deteriorated overnight, and the workload for today was heavy. There were four other doctors working in the unit today, but Dougie was the most senior and the most experienced. He could tell that Benedict was contemplating offering to stay.

'Go home,' he insisted, putting a hand on Benedict's shoulder. 'If things get hectic, I will call you.'

Benedict gave a grateful smile. 'I'm not going to argue. I'm just going to sleep.'

Dougie called the rest of the staff over to discuss the new arrivals and the patients who had deteriorated. He did a ward round, reassessing each patient, writing up new orders and leaving some specific instructions around care. It was complicated and he knew it. Some of the drugs being delivered by syringe pumps were to be amended on an hourly basis, dependent on the baby's observations.

He ordered some new investigations into a few other babies that he felt were deteriorating. He was so busy that it took him to around midday to take some time to take stock of the recent changes.

A horrible sensation drifted across him. A number of the babies who had previously done well in the unit had got worse in the last twenty-four to thirty-six hours. This wasn't unheard of. Any baby in a NICU could become sick at any point. Bleeding disorders, organ damage, breathing difficulties could all occur in premature babies. But the numbers last night just seemed unusual. It was setting off alarm bells in his head that he didn't like.

Dougie sat for a few minutes and tried to rationalise everything in his brain. Ignoring things was the easy option. The quiet option. But it would never be the right option for a practising physician.

He pulled up the rota and scanned it. With so many staff working here it was difficult to pick out any pattern. A few names jumped out at him, but he also wanted to be cautious. He looked across the NICU. A couple of those staff were on duty today.

As the doctor in charge, he could review any baby at any point. So he started doing a walk round. It had been four hours since the ward round and it wasn't unusual to do them more frequently in a unit like this.

The first few babies he reviewed were still very sick. Their medications and observations were all recorded. The next baby he reached was a little late for his observations. But he quickly saw the member of staff, dealing with an upset mother. Dougie checked over the baby himself and recorded the obs, adjusting the syringe driver and marking on the chart. The nurse looked over and gave him a grateful nod.

These kinds of things he understood. This wasn't someone being lazy or sloppy at work. This was a member of staff dealing with a crisis as it arose. He was quite sure that in another few minutes she would have likely asked a colleague to do the checks for her.

The next baby was midway through their checks. The nurse was away to make up a new syringe of medicine. He followed her into the treatment room, where she was on her phone. She had her back to him and clearly hadn't noticed him. She had the medicines in front of her and was reconstituting while she spoke angrily into the phone.

Dougie was instantly unhappy. She was preparing a syringe of diuretics and also a new IV containing fluids with potassium. Two extremely vital medicines that had to be monitored with precision. A wrong button pressed or a wrong calculation could be fatal for a baby.

Two seconds later she was yelling at the person at the end of the phone. As she did so, she pressed some buttons on the IV infusion pump. Dougie knew instantly they were wrong. They might be in the treatment room, not connected yet to any patient, but the apparent mistake was enough to make the red mist descend.

'Nurse Lawson, would you get off your phone, please?'

His voice boomed across the treatment room and the nurse jumped. She spun around, her face reddening as she said a final few words and cut the call.

She started to speak but he held up his hand.

'You know the rules. Phones in the coffee room only.' He held his hand out to the counter and walked over to look at the vial of medicine she'd been reconstituting. Although she had mixed it, she hadn't yet recorded the date, time or her initials. All of which were an essential part of mixing a medicine.

He held up the vial and pointed to the empty space.

'You interrupted me,' she started angrily, but Dougie wasn't having it.

'I interrupted your call. You'd already re-constituted the medicine. And what about this?' He turned and pointed at the IV infusion pump.

She blinked, indignation on her face. Then looked again, and paled.

'You know that's the wrong rate.'

She didn't speak. Her mouth was slightly open. He could almost see the cogs turning in her brain, wondering why on earth she'd pressed the wrong numbers. He knew this had never been deliberate. But if she'd connected that infusion without changing the rate he didn't even want to contemplate what might have happened.

Alice walked through the door. She'd changed her scrubs three times. Bright pink, purple and then pale pink—all just seemed to emphasise the large purple bruising around her neck. She'd done her best to disguise it in part with foundation. But it was still there—and still visible. So she'd finally settled on a pale blue pair with multicoloured tiny teddy bears all over them in the hope that people's eyes would be drawn to the tiny bears rather than her neck.

She already knew it wouldn't work.

A few of her colleagues literally met her at the door, giving her a hug and all telling her she'd come back to work much too soon. Her stomach was already in knots. Not from being back to work. She felt safe here—and perfectly capable of doing her job. She'd agreed with Tara only to work four hours today, on the understanding that if she felt unwell at any point she could go home.

But where was home now? She'd spent the last two nights with Penny and Benedict. They'd been perfect hosts but she was invading their privacy and she knew it. Her home was in Foggy Bottom. The townhouse she'd always been so proud of and loved living in. Did she still feel that way? To be honest, she wasn't sure. She wouldn't really know until she went back.

The reason her stomach was in knots was the fact she knew that Dougie was working today. Everything felt up in the air. She'd met a guy she'd worked with, moved in with and fallen in love with, all at breakneck speed. There had been tiny reservations deep down

inside. The trust stuff was hard. She'd realised her history had affected her more than
she'd ever admitted. But she still had the underlying feeling that Dougie hadn't put all his
cards on the table either. He hadn't hesitated
for a second when he'd seen her in trouble—
she'd known that about him, anyway. But the
hurt in his eyes had been evident when he'd
realised she hadn't trusted him enough to tell
him about her stalker returning. But part of
that time she hadn't been sure herself—and
if she'd told him she was worried she would
just have sounded paranoid.

The last couple of days there had been only
a few texts. She didn't want to text him. She
wanted to *see* him. *Talk* to him.

And today would be that day. She scanned
the unit but couldn't see him. He could be
anywhere. He could be away for a break, or
called to another part of the hospital if there
was an emergency, or in the coffee room or
the office.

Jake, the new NICU nurse, came over next
to her. 'How are you feeling, Alice? I was
shocked when I heard what happened to you.'

He winced as he looked at her neck. 'What
is wrong with people?' He shook his head.
'I'm glad that you are safe. I'm covering Ruby

and Ryan today. I have a few questions; do you mind?'

She shook her head in relief. 'Not at all,' she said. 'I've been with them since they were admitted, so ask away.'

They moved over to the incubators. Ruby and Ryan both looked well and Angie was sitting in the corner, chatting easily with Indira. Things were obviously working out how everyone had hoped. Jake pulled up the electronic chart, alongside a few tests results.

'Okay,' he said, 'I was just wondering…'

Raised voices were heard from the treatment room and literally everyone in the unit froze. In a place that was normally very quiet they were extremely noticeable and Alice recognised one of the voices immediately— Dougie. He wasn't shouting. But he was telling someone in no uncertain terms that they hadn't followed procedures.

It took her a few seconds to recognise the other voice. Jill Lawson—she'd worked here for a few months. Alice didn't know her that well, but had always found her fine.

'What on earth is going on?' she asked Jake.

'I have no idea. Sounds like she hasn't done what she should have.' He gave her a sideways glance. 'After what Dr MacLachlan experienced back in London, you can't blame him for being a stickler for details.'

It was like a cold breeze blowing over her skin and making every hair stand on end.

'What do you mean?'

Jake looked confused, his brow furrowed. 'Aren't you two an item?'

'What's that got to do with anything?'

Now Jake looked distinctly uncomfortable. 'Well, surely it's come up?'

'What?' There was a determined edge to Alice's voice. When she was met with silence, she added, 'I suggest you let me know.' She glanced towards the treatment room, where the voices were continuing. 'And quickly.'

Jake ran a hand through his hair. 'It's just… that Dr MacLachlan was the person who first raised suspicions about Kayla Bates—you know the nurse in England who was convicted of trying to deliberately harm her patients.' He closed his eyes for a second, then said, 'Her NICU patients.'

He took another breath. 'Listen, I'm sorry. Because you and he are…you know, dating, I just assumed that this would have been something you'd talked about.'

Alice rocked back on her heels, reaching out and touching the surface nearest to her, which was one of the incubators. Of course she'd heard about the case. It had horrified her. But it had taken place in another country, so she hadn't pored over the details. She just remembered the nurse had gone to prison. She shook her head. 'I didn't think he worked there.'

Jake was quick to clarify, 'Oh, he didn't work at the hospital where the actual events happened. He worked at the one before. And it was him that had flagged her practice before she moved. They unpicked the whole story about her.' He glanced at the treatment room again. 'I worked at the unit after Dr MacLachlan had left. Word on the street was that he'd been really upset about things.' Jake bit his lip. 'I also heard that staff had initially been quite off with him when he'd suggested something might be wrong—though by the time I got there they were all claiming to have noticed things about her.'

Alice straightened her shoulders. She could see people in the unit looking at each other—wondering who should intervene on the raised voices.

'Let me handle this,' she said as she started towards the treatment room.

Jake put a hand gently on her arm. 'Are you sure? I could do this. I might not know Dougie, but I do know the history.'

Alice appreciated the offer. 'You just got here, Jake. Let me sort the trouble out.'

She took some swift steps to the treatment room and walked in just as Jill was clearly about to launch into another diatribe. Her face was red and blotchy, and she was clearly furious. She was also clutching her mobile phone in one hand.

Dougie, in contrast, looked icily calm. Although his voice had been raised it was steady, with a real no-nonsense tone. He wasn't going to let this go.

'Enough.' She raised both hands as she walked in. Both turned at the same time and she could see the simultaneous flinching at the sight of her neck. But Alice had a job to do. 'Your voices can be heard outside. You're disturbing the unit that we strive hard to keep as a calm and peaceful place.' She turned first to Jill. 'Tell me what has happened.'

Dougie tried to talk first, but she kept one hand lifted to him. Jill was clearly worked up and nervous. 'He disturbed me while I was making up a medicine—then complained I hadn't signed and dated it.' She shot him a fierce look. 'Then he said I'd put the wrong number into the IV infusion pump, but I'm nowhere near a patient and it isn't connected.

I don't see why any of this is his business.'
She folded her arms and tilted her chin up.

Alice turned around to face Dougie. 'Dr
MacLachlan, would you like to tell me your
side?'

She saw something flash in his eyes. She
knew it was her use of his formal title, but in
this situation that was entirely correct.

'Nurse Lawson was on her phone while she
was in the treatment room. She wasn't paying attention to what she was doing, which is
clear by the fact she reconstituted the medicine but didn't initial and date and time it.
Then she put the incorrect dosage and rate
into the IV infusion pump. It might have not
reached a patient, but it was about to. Her
mind wasn't on the job. Careless mistakes
like this can cost lives.'

There was a tic around his jawline. He was
angry. Was it possible he was even angrier
than he'd been the other night? This was a
whole new side of Dougie she'd never seen.

She was looking at a new man. One with a
whole history he hadn't revealed to her. That
hurt. She hadn't even had time to process
what Jake had told her outside—there would
be time for that later.

For Alice this was like playing devil's advocate. Jill started again, but Alice stopped

her. 'Enough. Jill. Were you on your phone in the treatment room?'

Jill's face was so red she looked as though she might burst. 'Yes, but—'

'Is there an emergency? Do you need to go home?'

She was being concise and to the point. Jill knew the rules. But Alice had to establish if something unusual had happened that might explain why Jill had taken a call.

Now Jill's jaw was clenched, as if she was contemplating what to answer. She must have known that Alice had just given her a get-out clause. Would she take it?

'No,' she admitted. 'I'm having issues at home and we were having a fight.'

Alice made herself clear. 'Do you need some time out? Is your home life affecting your work life?'

Jill didn't answer, so Alice stepped over and put a hand on Jill's arm. 'Jill, do you feel safe? Is there anything we can do to help you?'

But Jill gave her a grateful smile and shook her head. 'No, it's nothing like that. Thanks for asking.' She looked at Dougie. 'I shouldn't have answered my phone, but I haven't done anything wrong and you've got no right to say I have.'

Alice cut in. 'Actually, Jill, in this unit it's everyone's job to make sure our colleagues are doing things correctly. While we know we are all responsible for our own practice, I would expect any member of staff to question something that they thought was wrong, before there could be a patient incident.'

She moved over and lifted the vial. 'This one isn't signed and dated, so will have to be destroyed. Jill, I want you to record that in the stock items and I'll countersign it with you.'

She still hadn't let Dougie speak. She could sense his eyes on her. But she was doing her best to be fair to both parties. Alice put her hand on the infusion. 'Which patient is this for?'

Jill told her.

'And what's the correct dosage for that patient, based on their weight?'

Dougie rattled it off automatically. Alice knew it too. She'd worked here so long it was practically ingrained in her brain. The current figures on the display were three times the normal dose and it made her feel physically sick.

Alice breathed. She wasn't in charge of this unit. Tara was, and she would report back to Tara later. Right now, she was acting as mediator. But she knew how things should

go in this environment. The words 'support-
ive conversation' circulated in her brain. She
couldn't be confrontational.

'Jill, can you tell me what's happened here?'

Jill looked at the figures again. It was clear
she was trying to find the words. 'I don't
know,' she admitted. 'I don't know why I put
that in. I know the correct dosage.'

Alice laid a gentle hand on her arm. 'Okay.'
She turned to face Dougie. 'Dr MacLachlan,
I understand your concerns and thank you for
raising them. If you can leave us alone right
now, Jill and I will ensure the medicines are
prepared correctly and everything is counter-
signed and double-checked before it reaches
the patient.' She took another breath and kept
her voice steady. 'As with any potential errors
in NICU, we will record this on the electronic
system as a near miss.'

Dougie looked at her. She could tell immediately he wasn't finished and there was so
much more simmering beneath the surface.
And now she knew and understood what that
was. But she had to be fair. She had no reason
to suspect anything other than human error.
The mistake had been caught and could be
remedied with no harm done. Lessons would
be learned from today. He continued to stand
there.

She lifted her chin. 'Dr MacLachlan, you and I can discuss this later. However, Nurse Lawson and I have a patient to attend to.' She took one step forward and glanced out to the unit. Jake was standing over Jill's current patient, taking a new set of observations. All was well.

Dougie turned on his heel and walked out.

Jill promptly burst into tears. Alice's head was throbbing. But, no matter how unwell she felt right now, she was glad she had come in today. She'd learned something she needed to know. The information hadn't come to her in the way it should have—and it was up to her to deal with it now.

'Do you feel as if you can continue?' Alice asked gently.

Jill was breathing quickly. 'I can't believe I made a mistake like that. What if he hadn't come in? You know I would have checked again before I connected the IV, don't you? Please tell me that you do.'

Alice nodded. 'I understand you were distracted. I understand you were upset. Let's just do everything by the book, get your patient's medicines restarted, then we can sit together and fill in the near miss record. We are all human, Jill. But let's just remember that no harm was done today.'

Jill's breathing steadied and she swallowed and gave a nod. 'Okay. Thank you.' She glanced over her shoulder. 'I just wish Dr MacLachlan would remember that too.'

Alice pressed her lips together. She wanted to say the words—that he was human too.

But right now she just didn't feel she could. It felt disloyal to Jill, and she was trying to hide the fact that she was angry with him for not telling her the truth.

She kept her voice even. 'Okay, let's get this sorted,' she said to Jill, and they started to check the prescriptions again.

Dougie was pacing. He couldn't help it. He'd done some other checks in the unit and, after a few curious glances from others, had taken himself into the office. Alice seemed to be taking an age. He hated the fact that other concerns were still floating in his head.

He still had questions about the number of kids who'd become sick in the last couple of days, and he knew nothing would satisfy with him without there being some kind of review.

The image that was sticking in his brain right now, though, was the vivid purple around Alice's throat. It was angry, it screamed trauma; he could swear he could see the mark of fingers. It made him feel physically sick that someone had done that to her.

He also knew exactly how brave she was to come back to work and not hide away at home. It was almost like a sign of defiance and that was exactly what he would expect from Alice. She was nobody's victim.

Before he had a chance to think any further she opened the office door and sat down. She was carrying a cup of water and some headache pills in her hand, which she quickly swallowed. 'Why didn't you tell me?' she asked.

He sat back in his chair. 'Why didn't I tell you what?'

'Don't play games with me, Dougie. Why didn't you tell me about your experiences back in London—about that Kayla nurse?'

His throat was dry. Jake must have told her. It was the only thing that made sense right now.

He spoke steadily. 'I didn't tell you because I don't like to talk about it at all. I worked with someone who went on to try and harm children. I raised concerns about her and was made to feel as if I had victimised her. We had no idea where she'd gone, and the first time we found out about everything was when the police turned up to ask questions.'

Alice licked her lips. She kept her brown eyes fixed on his. 'I can't imagine how horrible that was. But that doesn't explain why you didn't trust me enough to tell me. It might have helped me understand why you seemed to double-check what other staff were doing. Everyone had noticed you doing it.'

Dougie closed his eyes for a few seconds and sighed. It didn't matter that he'd tried to temper his instincts. It really hadn't worked.

She continued. 'That with Jill today?'

'She could have done something very wrong,' he interrupted.

'You're right,' she said. 'She could have. But getting into a fight with a member of staff is not how we do things around here. You could have handled things differently.'

'These things have to be handled at the time. We can't just wait and let something happen.'

'I agree,' she said. 'But…' She chose her words carefully in light of what she now knew. 'But we have to assume that a member of staff made a mistake and treat them with compassion and respect. I'm sure that Jill won't sleep a wink tonight. You could have spoken to her differently. I know that you're passionate about this, but not every staff member is trying to do deliberate harm.'

The words came out and hung in the air between them.

Dougie studied her closely. 'And there,' he said after a pause, 'is the elephant in the room.'

'What do you mean?' Alice snapped. She was getting more irritable. She was tired, her head still ached and all she really wanted to do was go home.

She couldn't understand what was wrong that Dougie couldn't have told her what had happened before. Did she seem judgemental? Or unsympathetic? She wouldn't have thought so, but now she couldn't think straight and felt paranoid.

'You should have told me,' she said, completely exasperated. 'You didn't have faith in me.'

'And you didn't have faith in me.' It was like some weird kind of tit-for-tat.

They sat looking at each other and Alice shifted in her seat. Of course. She hadn't told Dougie about herself; why should he reveal part of himself to her?

'That was different.'

'Why?'

She waved a hand. 'Because it was about life, not work. I thought you might have judged me for being on so many dating apps. And you might have thought I'd done something to encourage him.'

Dougie's brow wrinkled. 'Why on earth would you think that?'

She shook her head. 'Because everything was new between us. It was going so well, and I didn't want anything to spoil it.'

'Ditto,' he said softly.

'What?'

'I came to a new place. Met a new girl— a great girl. I came here with the purpose of leaving the past behind me. I didn't trust my own judgement any more. But you didn't know any of that, and I,' he said slowly, 'didn't want to do anything to spoil it.'

Something pinged in her brain. 'Why didn't you trust your own judgement?'

Dougie leaned forward, clasping his hands over his knees. Now he wasn't looking at her. 'Because before anything happened—' he ran his hands through his hair '—I'd gone on a date with Kayla.'

Oh, dear. Alice's stomach clenched in a horrible, cringing and jealous kind of way.

'You dated her?' She couldn't help the words—it was just a natural reaction.

Dougie looked up at her through his dark hair. 'Once. We went on a date once. And I just had a weird feeling about everything and it never happened again.'

But you still went on a date with her. Alice didn't repeat the words out loud, but they reverberated around her brain.

He shook his head. 'Then everything got horribly complicated. She was very friendly, in everyone's faces. People thought she was great. And when I noticed things at work and mentioned it, people automatically jumped to her defence. Then someone new started at work. And they'd been at the place she'd worked previously. A few questions were asked, and some of the more senior staff took me seriously. Kayla eventually did something wrong and was put on supervised practice. But by that point she was telling people I had a vendetta against her as she'd refused to go on a second date with me.'

'Yikes,' said Alice and she sagged a little in her chair. She bit her lip for a moment. 'You must have been popular.'

He raised his eyebrows, then gave a slow nod. 'You can imagine.' He sat back up properly. 'She left, went to another job, didn't ask for references. Our manager reported her to the nursing governing body, but nine months later the police came visiting because of what had happened at her new post.'

Alice frowned. 'So, why did you leave? Nothing happened on your watch.'

He groaned. 'But it could have. And it made me feel paranoid about everyone around about me. Were they happy and friendly because they were trying to distract from the fact they might be trying to do harm?'

Alice looked at him. 'Is that what you honestly thought about the people you worked with?' She looked out of the office door. 'The people here?' She paused and swallowed, putting her hand on her chest. 'Me?'

Dougie opened his mouth to speak but paused and that made her heart twist inside her chest.

'No…yes…maybe. Not you. Definitely not you. But it made me cautious in general. It made me question everything, particularly my own judgement. After all, I went on a date with her. What does that say about me? And I became really obsessed with procedures and protocols and making sure they were followed correctly.'

Alice's heart was still twisting inside her chest. 'Well, they're there for a reason. We should follow them. I think everyone does.'

'But do you *know*?' The response was instant and if she'd been standing next to him she would have jumped. Dougie sunk his head into his hands. 'My former boss told me I needed a change of scene,' he admitted. He looked back at her. 'He was right. And I thought it would help.'

'But it hasn't?'

His expression was pained. 'When I came in today I noticed that the rate of babies getting sick over the last couple of days is much higher than normal.'

Alice was horrified. She'd been off the last two days, so hadn't noticed. 'You think something is happening here? Is that why you snapped at Jill?'

She couldn't help it. She was automatically defensive of the place she'd worked in and loved for the last five years.

When he didn't say anything it was as if a little part of her died inside.

She took another breath, wondering how to stay calm. But it was clear Dougie had already made a decision.

'Maybe you think it's nothing—and you could be right. But I have to mention this. I have to raise the issue of the number of babies being unwell in such a short space of time.' He put a hand on his chest. 'It could be I'm paranoid. But I've run a few numbers, a few stats, because that's what I do. We are way over the average of where we should be. It could just be an anomaly, and these things happen. But as a professional? I feel responsible to ask Benedict and Tara to sit down and take a look at things. We have to review processes and reach a rational, researched decision that we are confident everything in the unit is working the way it should—and that includes the staff.'

Alice stood up. 'But my sister works here, and Benedict; do you suspect them too? Do you judge everyone by Kayla's standards?'

She couldn't help it. This whole place was family to her, not just Penny and Benedict. It was as if he was finding fault and trying to apportion blame. Her head just couldn't think straight. She put her hand over her heart. 'And what about me, Dougie? Are you investigating me too? Do you wonder if I've done anything? And does what we've had these last few weeks mean nothing to you? Or do you still not trust your judgement?' It was a low blow, but she couldn't help it.

Dougie looked at her with pained eyes. 'You haven't been here, Alice. You've been at home. But yes, if you had been here, then you, as well as me, and every other member of staff on duty, need to be fed into the details gathered around the events in the last few days.'

She froze. Hating that was how his brain was working. Tears formed in her eyes. 'This is a good place,' she whispered.

Dougie held her gaze with his steady blue eyes. 'And good places are not afraid of reviews. They're not afraid to cross every t, dot every i, evidence everything to make sure care is of a consistent high standard.'

He made it all sound so reasonable, so rational—even though he hadn't been acting that way earlier. But she couldn't keep her emotions in check. She wished she hadn't insisted on coming in today. But maybe this was always meant to happen. Maybe she had to see his reaction today, and all the events, to understand that she really didn't know this man at all. What she hadn't reckoned on was how much it would break her heart.

She'd never really known Dougie at all.

She put her hand on her heart. 'What were we even doing?' she asked softly.

'What?'

She shook her head. 'Us. This.' She pointed her fingers back and forth between them. 'This isn't about work. This is about us, and the fact that neither one of us trusted the other enough to tell them what we should.'

She swallowed, her throat aching. 'I was scared I would ruin things if I told you about the stalker.' Her voice was shaky. 'And it sounds like you felt the same way about revealing your history to me.'

Dougie breathed slowly. 'It's just a horrible story. I came here to get away from that. I came here to start afresh. It's haunted me. It's made me paranoid at work. It's made me not trust my own judgement.'

'And that includes me, doesn't it?'

He opened his mouth to speak and then paused, dipping his head. When he finally raised his gaze he whispered, 'I want to trust you, but I don't even trust myself. How can I really trust anyone again?'

A tear rolled down her cheek. 'I want to shout. I want to scream. But... I get it. Because I couldn't let go the fact that I knew you were keeping something from me. I didn't want to lose my heart to someone I couldn't fully trust. So I always had to hold something back.'

They stared at each other in silence, both realising they'd reached the point of no return. Without trust, there was nothing—no foundation to build on.

'I need to go home.' That was all that could come out right now from Alice.

Dougie's eyes flashed with worry. 'I understand.'

Alice drew herself up as strongly as she could. 'No, you don't.' With every second, she prayed that her voice wouldn't break. 'I need to be alone.'

Dougie blinked; she could see him processing her words.

'I can't be around you. Not while you're thinking like this. Not when you look around and see people who want to do harm, rather than people who are here to do a good job and save lives. You need to talk to someone about this, Dougie. The fact that those thoughts are always in your mind isn't healthy. It makes me think that I never really knew you at all. Just like you didn't know me. We were pretending with each other. We were pretending that we were honest with each other and that we might have a chance at making things work. But all this?' She held out her hands first of all, and then they went almost by compulsion to her neck. She shook her head. 'If we can't be honest with each other, how can we be anything else?' Her voice was deep and scratchy now. 'Please find somewhere else to stay. I think it's for the best.'

He stood there for a moment, not saying anything. Not fighting for her. Not fighting for them. That told her all she really needed to know.

'I'll stay someplace else tonight and arrange to pick up my things tomorrow.'

It came out so matter-of-fact. As if nothing that had just happened had made any impact on him at all.

So Alice turned, left the office, said goodbye to Jake and left the unit. She collected her things from the locker room and made it all the way to the subway before she started sobbing.

CHAPTER TEN

DOUGIE SAT IN the room with Benedict, Tara, the hospital medical director, an independent auditor, a clinical governance expert and someone from another NICU in Washington.

The hospital director started. 'We have agreed to gather here today to review the evidence we have for a one- to two-day period when a number of babies became unexpectedly sick in NICU. We all understand these incidents can happen, due to the vulnerable nature of these patients. However, this was raised by Dr MacLachlan as a potential anomaly—one which we know would have been highlighted at a national level at some point—and we welcome the chance to do a review of the circumstances of each of these patients and take into account all factors which could be an influence.'

Sitting at his left elbow were electronic prescribing records, the staff rota, all tests ordered and reviewed and medical records for every case. 'We have seventeen patients to review. Is everyone agreed with how we will carry out this review, and record and report our findings?'

There was a murmur of assent around the table. Both Benedict and Tara looked worried. But as soon as Dougie had raised concerns about the issue both had agreed the spike in numbers was odd and it would be good to review.

He was feeling strangely acknowledged now, that things weren't just in his head and he hadn't been paranoid and overreacting. But, while that might give some professional reassurance, no one could argue that his personal life wasn't a complete and utter mess.

He'd lost the one true thing he'd finally found. Alice.

His heart felt as if it had been put through a shredder. The look on her face, her upset and confusion haunted him. He'd wanted to text or phone her so many times. But he knew he'd disappointed her.

All he could remember was the vivid purple marks on her throat. At a point in their relationship where he should have been doing everything possible to protect her, love her and reassure her, he'd let her down badly. He had no idea how he could make amends for this. But he knew he wanted to. He'd never been so sure of anything in his life. Alice Greene well and truly had his heart.

He'd spent the first night in one of the on-call rooms. He'd spent the next night at Benedict and Penny's. If he'd ever wanted to experience the complete and utter loyalty between sisters he'd been introduced to it by Penny's wall of icy silence.

It was clear that Benedict hadn't thought before offering him a bed for the night. Or maybe he was trying to play devil's advocate. Whatever it was, he'd slept one night in a comfortable bed but knew he had to find something else. Last thing he wanted to do was cause an argument between two people he respected and liked.

Some of the staff at work had been a little frosty. Others had been fine. One of the more junior staff had asked if they could look at some data for the review. It turned out he was a bit of a data geek and wanted to do some stats. It was an idea Dougie would have liked to embrace but he didn't want to overstep, so he'd just mentioned the offer to Benedict.

As he sat, the hospital director pushed around some files and once he opened them and saw the charts he tried not to smile. It seemed that Benedict had taken up the offer and before them was a clear table for each child with times, medicines, interventions and observations charted. There was further work with timelines running over each other to show if there were any correlations when babies had started to deteriorate. It was actually a remarkable piece of work.

The director gave a nod. 'This is only preliminary data to give us a starting point for our review. If we decide we need to investigate further, then we can ask an independent advisor to do that work for us.'

Dougie was already scanning and his heart was lightening. They'd be here for hours, but he already got a sense that there was no glaring causal factor. He couldn't begin to say how good that felt. These were people he'd got to know and really like over the last couple of months. He didn't want to think ill of anyone, but he had a responsibility as a neonatologist to always put his patients first. He just hoped others would understand that.

Particularly Alice. He wanted to let his mind drift. He wanted to imagine all the ways he could try to say sorry. Let her know that he still loved her. More than anything he wanted a chance for them to be together again. What he didn't know was how Alice might respond.

But, here and now, he had to concentrate. He had to see through this investigation and accept whatever the results were.

Then he could start trying to rebuild his life again.

CHAPTER ELEVEN

ALICE WAS MISERABLE. It had been three days since her heartbreaking conversation with Dougie and she'd taken some emergency annual leave. Tara had been wonderful—even though Alice appreciated that she must be under a whole host of stress herself. Tara was supporting Jill through the near miss, and also attempting to run a unit where all members of staff knew that questions were being asked and an investigation was pending.

Sooty gave a loud meow and padded over Alice's face again. Anything for attention. She wasn't quite sure what the cat wanted. As soon as Sooty had realised that Dougie hadn't come home the last few nights it was as if it was entirely her fault.

He'd hissed at her earlier when she'd been a little late filling the food bowl. When Alice had come up the stairs earlier, Sooty was lying at the entrance of what had originally been Dougie's room, with an expression on his face that could freeze over a blazing fire. She definitely wasn't popular, even in her own house!

Alice stood up and walked through to the bathroom. The purple had faded slightly and now had streaks of yellow. She hated it. George had phoned yesterday and let her know that, after her ex was arrested, he was subsequently detained, charged and refused bail, due to three other women coming forward with a range of complaints. Now, they just had to wait for his trial.

Alice walked back down the stairs and took up position on the sofa again. There was a dent in the sofa next to her where Dougie had started to leave an imprint with his larger frame.

Most of his things were still upstairs. It was clear he hadn't found somewhere permanent to stay yet, and she hated the way that made her heart happy. When she walked past his room she could still smell remnants of his aftershave.

The last three nights had been hard. At first she'd thought it was because she was in the house by herself. But the noises and creaks had been comforting rather than alarming. Maybe it was because she knew Dave was safely behind bars that she wasn't nervous in the way she'd been before. But having her own feeling of security left her with a huge Dougie-shaped hole in her life.

A tiny part of her had wondered if she'd been clinging onto Dougie for the wrong reasons—because she was nervous and felt threatened and didn't want to be home alone. Yes, Dougie had certainly made her feel safe and secure. But if she didn't need that now, if she wasn't scared any more, why did she still miss those, as well as other aspects of him being around?

Alice sighed as Sooty gave her another disgusted glance before strutting away with his tail in the air. She missed Dougie because she loved him. She loved all aspects of him—his baking, the way he hugged her, the way he made her laugh, his accent, even his slightly crabbit nature. All those little pieces built up the man she'd unexpectedly grown to love.

She hadn't been looking for any of this and it had just landed on her lap out of the blue. And she'd let it slip through her fingers.

She'd spent the last few days picking apart those few hours in the unit. Every bone in her body knew he'd been right to raise flags. Her colleague had done something wrong, not followed protocol and could have accidentally harmed a baby. Even though Alice liked Jill, she always knew that if Dougie hadn't intervened, Jill could have gone ahead and connected the IV pump without rechecking the rate because she'd been distracted—it didn't even bear thinking about. Jill could never have lived with a mistake like that. It would have destroyed her. So Dougie's actions had not only saved a baby, they had likely saved Jill too.

Alice had been full of emotion and reacted defensively around Dougie. She wished she'd paused. She wished she'd taken more time to think things through—maybe even even discussed it with Penny before telling him he had to move out.

She might as well have wrenched her own heart clean out of her chest. Because when it came down to the bones of it, they just hadn't trusted each other enough. She felt to blame—even though she knew the blame was equal.

Why had she let Dave impact her life so much? Why couldn't she have had enough assurance and confidence to write him off as the bad guy he'd been? She'd put barriers in place that were tough to try and shift. Would she ever get the chance again, and learn to trust someone?

She also knew that Dougie was currently assisting with the investigation. Benedict and Penny had both mentioned how worried they were. They all knew that a rapid rise in stats for their unit should be picked apart to make sure everything was functioning as it should.

Alice had been sending up silent prayers for the last few nights that, even though it would be unusual, all of these anomalies were merely coincidence.

She loved her unit; she was proud of it. Dougie had fitted in well. For a time he'd appeared to thrive, working alongside her. He was a good doctor. He was quick to spot any deterioration in their tiny patients and put plans in place. Being thorough was never a bad thing, and now it felt as if she'd judged him too harshly.

Her doorbell rang and she jumped in surprise. She wasn't expecting anyone. She pushed away the few milliseconds of panic and relaxed her shoulders and walked to the door, glancing through the peephole.

All she could see was orange.

She pulled back, blinked and looked again. Yip, orange.

She opened the door.

Dougie, with the biggest bunch of orange gerberas that she'd ever seen.

He looked nervous. He was wearing a leather jacket and jeans. 'Can we talk?'

She was still stunned that he was there and as she stood in silence he pushed the flowers towards her. She took them and gave a delayed nod, standing aside to let him come in.

He paced for a few moments before she said, 'Sit down,' trying to keep her face blank as he immediately sat in the Dougie-sized space on her sofa. He couldn't know that she'd sat with her hand on that space last night.

She grabbed a vase from under the sink, filled it with water and put the orange gerberas in the vase. He'd remembered. He'd remembered what she'd told him was her favourite flower. She had no idea where he'd got them in the city, but she was still struck by his thoughtfulness.

'How was the investigation?'

He leaned forward, resting his elbows on his knees. 'It was…good. All the data was examined. We are officially a statistical anomaly.'

'We are?' She was smiling now as relief surrounded her like a giant cloak.

He nodded. 'We are. There were a few tiny things picked up—but nothing that could have contributed to a deterioration in any child's condition.'

Alice sat down next to him. 'What things?'

He shook his head. 'Late recording of observations on occasions, late administration of medicines. A test being delayed. A blood result not being available because a sample was mislabelled.'

Alice nodded. She knew there were lots of reasons all of these things could happen. The unit was a busy place and if there was an immediate emergency—such as a cardiac arrest or intubation required—that had to take priority.

She breathed slowly. 'Anything else?'

He shook his head. What struck Alice most was how completely and utterly relieved Dougie was. He'd never wanted anything to be wrong at her unit.

'I know you had to raise your concerns,' she said slowly. 'And I was upset about it. I hated the fact that something might have been wrong in the place I loved and worked, and I couldn't be rational about it.'

'I know that,' he said easily. 'But our issues were never really to do with this.'

She looked at him steadily as he continued. 'I was angry that you didn't tell me about being stalked. I was annoyed you didn't trust me—even though I didn't really trust myself either. It seems ridiculous I could be upset about it.' He licked his lips and kept talking. 'And when you agreed to go home with Penny after being attacked... I just felt so useless.'

He held up a hand. 'I get she's your sister and you're close. I get you were attacked outside your house and it was perfectly natural to want to get some space. And when I say this out loud it seems entirely rational.' He gave a gentle smile. 'But I guess I just can't be rational when it comes to you, Alice.' He shook his head. 'I wanted to protect you. I wanted to look after you. Now I feel like a Neanderthal man saying that out loud. You hadn't told me about Dave, you just wanted to get away from me, and I just thought... I'd imagined what I thought we had together.'

Alice could hardly breathe. She reached out and touched his hand. 'When you encouraged me to go with Penny I thought you didn't really love me. I knew you would be angry I hadn't told you about Dave, and it felt like you weren't prepared to fight for me. Then, after our words in the unit when I found out all about what happened back in England, I just couldn't make sense of what we were to each other. How can we be anything to each other if neither of us knows how to trust?'

He looked down at her hand, then back

up into her eyes. 'I made a mistake. I should have trusted you from the start and told you about England. And not fighting for you? Alice, I wanted to fight the world for you. But you'd just been through a traumatic experience and your sister clearly thought the best place for you was with her. You were vulnerable enough. And yes I was angry, but not really at you—at myself mainly for not being there when he attacked you. I wanted to respect the fact you might have needed space and some time with your sister to feel safe. I wanted to argue—but I thought that made me some kind of selfish monster.' His blue eyes fixed on hers. 'I'll never be that man. I love you, Alice. I want this to work between us. Tell me what I can do to fix it.'

She swallowed slowly and looked him in the eye. 'Anything?'

He didn't hesitate. 'Anything.'

She didn't hesitate either. 'Go to counselling. Talk through what happened and how it has made you wary of people—how at times you mistrust your colleagues without even wanting to. I know counselling might not be for a big Scottish guy like you. But I want you to try it. I want you to see if it can't take you out of that mindset.'

He gave her a soft smile and pulled a card

from his pocket. She looked at the name of the private counsellor, frowning in surprise. 'Where did you get this?'

'Indira. She was in with Angie again, came over, had a quiet word and gave me a recommendation.' He sighed. 'I was touched. And yes, my immediate response was to say no, but I took it, thanked her and made an appointment for next week.'

'You have?'

'I have.'

She squeezed his fingers tighter. 'You thought I wanted to be with my sister to feel safe. Penny will always be my confidante, my partner in crime and my best friend. But you're the one that I love, Dougie. You're the one that makes my heart sing, then break a moment later. You're the one that I want to wake up next to in the morning. You're the one that makes me feel safe.' She gave him a small smile. 'You're my happy ever after.' She put her other hand over their two clasping hands. 'I think we need to work at this together. I didn't tell you about Dave because I felt partly to blame—even though I wasn't. Then I felt as if I was imagining things.' She lifted her head and looked up. 'I guess I did what a lot of women do without realising it. I became a victim of myself. I shouldn't have doubted. I should have told you every-thing straight away. I have some work to do myself—' she put her hand on her chest '—because I don't want to feel like this, I shouldn't feel like this, but I let it happen.' She gave a slow nod. 'I won't let it happen again. Give me that card. I think I need it too. And if this person comes with Indira's recommendation, then that's good enough for me.'

He reached a hand over and cupped her cheek. 'Can we do this, Alice? Can we re-ally do this, and make this work between us? Because you are the only thing in this world that I want.'

She moved closer to him as Sooty ap-peared, meowing loudly and winding his way around Dougie's legs. They both laughed as Alice wrapped her hands around the back of Dougie's neck. 'Looks like I'm going to have to share you.'

'It's a lot to ask,' he said in the gruff Scot-tish accent she loved so much. 'But I guess I can make the sacrifice.' His lips hovered millimetres away from hers.

'I love you,' she whispered.

'I love you too.' Just as their lips were about to touch, a corny song started playing loudly from his pocket.

Laughter erupted. 'I know it!' squealed Alice. 'Miami Sound Machine. "Bad Boy" from *Three Men and a Baby*. I was always going to get that one. You got to play tougher than that.'

Dougie tossed his phone over his shoulder as it continued to play, and proceeded to pull her down onto the sofa to show her just how bad he could be.

EPILOGUE

BENEDICT AND PENNY had chosen the perfect setting. The hotel was on the outskirts of Washington, with beautiful gardens, chairs set on the lawn and a decorated floral archway where the registrant stood waiting.

Alice was more nervous than Penny. It was a relatively quiet wedding as Benedict didn't have a large family. Alice and Penny's mom and dad were there, along with many of the couple's friends from the hospital.

Alice stared out of the window of the large room above the gardens where Penny's hair was just getting some final touches. Benedict and Dougie, who was his best man, were already waiting under the archway, both dressed in smart suits.

'Come on, Penny,' said Alice nervously. 'Your groom is waiting.'

'All ready,' Penny said, smiling, the calmest woman in the room. She stood up in her slim gold dress and picked up her ivory flowers with a few gold ribbons.

Alice gave a little gasp. 'You look perfect,' she sighed, air-kissing her sister's cheek so she didn't spoil her make-up.

Penny gave a nervous laugh. 'Let's hope Benedict thinks so.'

A few moments later Alice walked down the aisle first in her coral dress, smiling as Dougie winked at her.

Penny followed on their father's arm, beaming the whole way. The sun shone brightly as they recited vows that they had written for each other, and their friends all cheered loudly as the registrant finally said the words, 'And now you may kiss the bride.'

Benedict didn't need to be told twice.

The relaxed feel of the wedding continued into the evening. Dougie held Alice's hand whenever one of them wasn't called to other duties.

The meal was finished, speeches completed and cake cut when Penny gave her friends a shout.

'Before myself and my husband—' there was a loud cheer and she smiled '—have our first dance, there's another tradition I want to fulfil. Come on over, ladies.'

Alice frowned. She hadn't remembered

this part, but as Penny stood in front of her friends, then spun around with her back to them, clutching her bouquet, Alice quickly caught on.

'One…' She started swinging her arms with the bouquet.

'Two!' shouted her friends.

By the time they reached three, the whole room had joined in.

But Penny stopped. She spun around again, a knowing smile on her face as she walked over to her sister and deliberately handed her the bouquet. Alice didn't understand until the woman next to her gasped and nudged her side.

She looked behind her. Dougie was down on one knee, looking entirely nervous. Her mom and dad stood smiling, arm in arm and clearly in on the surprise. Penny and Benedict came alongside her too.

Dougie let out a slow breath and held up the black box he had in one hand. 'Alice Greene, the woman I love and trust with my entire heart and every single cell in my body, will you do me the honour of being my wife?'

He lifted his other hand, which held a single orange gerbera.

She leaned forward and whispered in his

ear, 'I think you're supposed to open the box when you ask,' she teased.

'Darn it,' said Dougie in his thick Scottish accent, flicking the box open with his thumb.

The truth was, Alice wouldn't have cared if it had been a jelly ring in the box, but the square-cut emerald with a diamond on either side was stunning.

She wrapped her arms around his neck. 'Get up, dummy,' she said, grinning. 'Of course the answer is yes.'

The crowd let out a cheer around her as Dougie picked her up and swung her around.

Alice let out a squeal of delight, catching glimpses of Penny and Benedict, and her mom and dad, who had all clearly plotted with Dougie.

Their relationship had grown stronger and stronger in the last few months. Both of them had seen the counsellor and learned to unpick their deep-rooted feelings of mistrust. It had taken a little time, but they'd finally and joyously got there.

'Hey—' she grinned as he set her down '—does this mean I get to see you in a kilt and find out if the stories about Scotsmen are true?'

He kissed her thoroughly. 'Absolutely,' he

said in a voice only for her. 'How about I hire a kilt and start practising?'

Her smile widened. 'You know what they say…practice makes perfect.' And she laughed as he picked her up and spun her around again.

* * * * *

If you missed the previous story in the Neonatal Nurses duet, then check out

A Nurse to Claim His Heart
by Juliette Hyland

If you enjoyed this story, check out these other great reads from Scarlet Wilson

Marriage Miracle in Emergency
A Festive Fling in Stockholm
Reawakened by the Italian Surgeon

All available now!